·THE·
BREAD
WINNER

Also by Arvella Whitmore:
You're a Real Hero, Amanda

·THE· BREAD WINNER

ARVELLA WHITMORE

Houghton Mifflin Company
Boston 1990

Printed in the United States of America

BP 10 9 8 7 6 5 4 3 2 1

Library of Congress Cataloging-in-Publication Data

Whitmore, Arvella.
  The bread winner / Arvella Whitmore.
      p.   cm.
  Summary: When both her parents are unable to find work and pay the
bills during the Great Depression, resourceful Sarah Ann Puckett
saves the family from the poorhouse by selling her prizewinning
homemade bread.
  ISBN 0-395-53705-3
  [1. Depressions—1929—Fiction.   2. Family problems—Fiction.
3. Bakers and bakeries—Fiction.]   I. Title.
PZ7.W598Br   1990   90-33470
[Fic]—dc20   CIP
                             AC

To the Tuesday Writers' Group:
Bette Abdella, Nancy Bestul,
Agnes Houck, Judith King, Wanda Rauma,
and Joanne Reisberg

1

c h a p t e r

Excited and impatient, Sarah fidgeted in her seat between Mama and Daddy. Their furniture, piled high in back of their Model T truck, rattled as they bumped across the railroad tracks. Her parents had explained to Sarah that their house in town wouldn't be as nice as the one they'd had on the farm. But even so, she couldn't wait to see it.

Sarah soon noticed that they were headed straight into Waheegan's poorest section. Everyone called it Shantytown. This couldn't be where their new home was!

"Are you going the right way, Daddy?" she asked.

"Yes, Sarah," said her father. "We'll be there soon."

They were probably just passing through this part of town on their way to a better neighborhood, she thought. The newspaper Daddy had just bought was lying in his lap, fluttering noisily in the breeze. Sarah glanced at the front page. Under a picture of President Herbert Hoover a thick black headline read, HARD TIMES TO END SOON. Another said just the opposite: THE DEPRESSION DEEPENS. When she noticed the date in the upper right-hand corner, she smiled and bit her lip. So that's what Daddy was up to. It was April Fool's Day! The date, April 1, 1932, was there in plain sight. Her father would probably drive up to some shack and say, "This is it, Sarah." Then, after he laughed and said "April fool," they'd drive on to their real house.

She glanced at Daddy. He didn't look like someone about to play a joke on her. His hands were gripping the steering wheel so hard his knuckles had turned white. He looked worried. And his voice had sounded as if the words were being squeezed out of him.

Sarah glanced up at Mama. Her eyes were red. She had been crying off and on since they left the farm half an hour ago. Sarah had cried some, too, but now she felt excited about moving to town. There will be so many things to do here, she thought. There was a movie house downtown, the Aladdin, and there were stores that sold ice cream and candy and pretty dresses. And she'd be making lots of friends in her new neighborhood and school.

Sarah craned her neck to peer around her parents. The houses in this part of town looked terrible, she thought. Many had peeling paint or no paint at all. On one house the broken porch railing hung at a crazy angle, and part of it lay in the yard along with scattered trash. Some of the yards were covered with scraps of dirty cloth, pieces of toys, torn boxes, old tires, and rusty auto parts. Cardboard had been tucked into broken windows. She had always thought of Waheegan as a nice town. But she had never seen this part of it before.

Dirty and ragged children of all ages swarmed around their truck. Two, a boy and a girl, jumped onto their right running board and rode along with them.

2

"Where're you movin' to?" asked the girl. Her face was filthy and she had a runny nose. She looked about two years younger than Sarah. Ten, maybe.

"Are you gonna be livin' 'round here?" the girl asked. Sarah certainly hoped not. "I don't know," she said.

"Why are you wearin' them overalls?" asked the boy. "Are you from a farm?"

Sarah looked down at her pant legs. Maybe she should have worn one of the two dresses she'd packed away. But the fifteen-mile ride in their open truck had been chilly. Besides, her dresses had been mended and looked shabby. They hadn't bought new clothes for a long time because Daddy had been trying to save the farm and needed every penny.

"Children, please get off," cried Mama. "It isn't safe to ride on the truck like that."

"You can't make us!" yelled the boy. The nerve, thought Sarah. He and the girl looked alike with their broad faces, thick noses, and close-set eyes. Sarah glanced over her shoulder and saw other children hanging onto the truck. The ones who were unable to hitch a ride ran beside them in the street. The two jumped off the running board. Then the mob of children, hollering swear words, chased them for a few yards before turning back. Sarah hoped she'd seen the last of them.

As Daddy drove on another block or two, Sarah noticed that the houses looked worse, scarcely more than shacks. No larger or better built than some of the old outbuildings on their farm. And here the streets weren't paved, and there were no sidewalks.

3

Daddy stopped the truck in front of an unpainted shack that could have passed for their farm's machinery shed.

"Well, this is it," he said.

Sarah studied his face. From the expression in his eyes, she knew better than to ask if this was some kind of joke. He wore the same glassy-eyed look that had come over him when he realized he couldn't save their farm.

Daddy sighed, grasped Sarah's shoulders, and looked into her face. "I'm sorry, but this is where we'll have to live until your mother and I find work of some kind. Let's hope it won't be for long." Sarah swallowed the lump rising in her throat and fought back her tears.

Mama took her hand, opened the door, and pulled her out of the truck. "Let's go in and take a look." As they walked toward the shack, Sarah couldn't hold back the crying any longer. Mama's arms wrapped around her. "These are hard times for us, dear. We've tried to explain that to you. It's the Depression."

"But Mama! I didn't know we were this poor."

"The farm was all we had, Sarah, and now it's gone." Mama patted her back. "Just remember, honey. All that really matters is that we're healthy and together. And things will work out for us. I know they will. We won't be staying here long." Sarah buried her face in the softness of Mama's old coat and breathed in its woolly smell. From what her parents had said about the house, she knew it wouldn't be fancy, but never for a moment had she expected anything this bad.

"Look over there, Sarah." Mama pointed to trees in the distance. "The river's nearby, and we'll be able to go fishing

4

and hunting any time we feel like it." Her cheerful words couldn't mask the nervous break in her voice.

Daddy was still in the truck, resting his head against the steering wheel. He quickly straightened up and got out when their friend Mr. Miller drove up behind him with a wagon and team of horses. Mr. Miller had brought the rest of their furniture.

Still in shock, Sarah followed Mama, Daddy, and Mr. Miller to the house. While her father was unlocking the door, Sarah noticed a face peeking out at them from a tiny front window. It quickly disappeared.

"Daddy, somebody's in there."

"You're right, Sarah," said Mama. "I hear voices inside. Please don't open that door, Frank. Why don't we get the police?"

"It's all right, Lucy," said Daddy. "Sounds like a bunch o' kids to me. We'll shoo 'em away." Daddy opened the squeaky door. He and Mr. Miller stepped inside, followed by Sarah and Mama. Five grimy boys wearing oddly mismatched clothes stood in the tiny room near a potbellied stove. Sarah judged them all to be a year or two older than she was, thirteen or fourteen. There was a bottle on the floor half full of something that looked like strong tea.

"What're you doing here?" asked Daddy.

"What does it look like?" one answered in a cracked voice as he stomped out a cigarette on the floor.

"How dare you mash that cigarette on my floor," cried Mama. "I spent hours yesterday scrubbing so that we could move into a clean house!" The boy picked up the cigarette butt.

5

"All right, out." Daddy stood aside and pointed to the door. One of the boys leaned over to pick up the bottle.

"Leave that stuff where it is," said Daddy in the quiet, level voice he used with Sarah when he expected her to obey.

The boy froze, but another one turned to him. "Aw, go ahead, Fuzz. Take the booze. He can't do nothin'."

"Leave it," said Daddy. "Go. And don't come back."

The floor groaned and creaked as the boys filed out. The last one to leave turned around. "Thief," he yelled at Daddy.

"Don't you dare talk that way to my husband," Mama said angrily. "We'll call the police!"

"Go ahead," said one of the boys. "No cop is gonna come to this part of town. Besides, you ain't got no phone."

When they were gone Daddy shook his head, picked up the bottle, and emptied it onto the ground by the sagging steps. "Sassy toughs. I'd like to knock their heads together."

Sarah looked around in disbelief. Their farmhouse had been a palace compared to this place. Her tour of the rooms didn't take long; there were only three. And the walls were cracked and stained. How could they possibly live here? If only this was just a nightmare, and she could wake up on the farm, safe and happy. But Daddy and Mr. Miller had already started bringing in the furniture.

At dusk their things were all inside the house. In the front room Sarah opened a large cardboard carton full of her belongings. Where should she put them? Though they had sold most of their furniture at the auction, there was still too much for this tiny place. The dining room table had been jammed into a corner of the front room, with its leaves lying underneath on the floor. Mama and Daddy were busy piling the six matching chairs on the tabletop.

"We can hardly walk in this room for all the furniture," said Mama. "Maybe we should sell the dining room set."

"No," said Daddy. "We oughta keep it. After all, it belonged to your mother, and I know how you feel about it. Besides, we won't be stayin' here long. We'll soon be back in a decent house."

Mama hugged Daddy. "Thank you for saying that. I just know we'll come through this all right, Frank."

Daddy patted Mama on the back. "We'll both hafta work mighty hard to get back on our feet again. But we've been through tough times before, Lucy, and they've never stopped us yet."

Sarah felt comforted by her parents' words. They wouldn't be there long. She just knew it. She carried the cardboard box into the kitchen, where a narrow iron cot had been placed in one corner. This is where she would have to sleep since there was no space for the cot anywhere else. The front room was hardly big enough for the few chairs they had brought along. And her parents' double bed was crammed into the tiny room off the kitchen. Sarah's bedroom furniture had been sold, since there wasn't room for it. Her mother had promised to replace it when they moved into a larger house.

Sarah set the heavy box down on her cot and sat beside it. Across from her the big black cookstove stood against an inside wall, and the kitchen worktable sat near the center

7

of the room. That table and stove were like two old friends, she thought. She was glad they hadn't been sold.

Last year Sarah had learned to bake bread at a 4H meeting. She had practiced her dough kneading at home on that old table. She'd learned, too, just when to pull the golden loaves from the oven so they'd be perfect. At the county fair last fall, her bread had won first prize: a blue ribbon. Daddy had been so proud he'd called her his champ. Whatever happened, she thought, she'd never give up bread making. She loved the magic of the rising dough, and the yeasty smell of the loaves baking. She wondered if it was true that town people bought their bread at grocery stores. She had a lot to learn about town life.

Kneeling on the cot, Sarah reached into the carton and pulled out a small wooden box. She called it her lucky box. Dried salted codfish had come in it once, and it had a handy sliding top. She opened it to admire once again the shiny ribbon she had won at the county fair.

After a supper of home-canned meat and vegetables brought from the farm, Sarah got up to fill another glass with water from the sink. She wasn't thirsty, but she loved turning the faucet on and watching the water pour into her glass. Not having to go outside to use a pump was one improvement over country life, she thought. Of course they had only cold water. No separate hot water faucet like most houses in town had. But they'd always heated their water on the stove anyway. She'd hoped for a bathroom, since most houses in town had one. But in this awful neighborhood, people still used outhouses.

Mama and Daddy sat at the kitchen table reading the newspaper.

"Are you finding anything in the help wanted ads?" asked Mama.

"Not really," Daddy said. "Most of 'em call for people with experience. Here's one for a bookkeeper. 'Experienced person only,' it says."

"But you kept our farm books," said Mama. "That's experience."

"Well, Lucy, farm books may not be the same. There's a creamery here in town, and I understand something about milk and cream. I could go and talk to them. And there's a flour mill here, too. I could see about a job there."

"You'll find something, Frank," said Mama. "I know you will."

"Well, Lucy, with this Depression it may not be easy, but I won't give up."

There they go again, thought Sarah. Her parents were always talking about the Depression. But so was everyone else. When wheat prices dropped down to twenty-five cents a bushel, the farmers all blamed the Depression. So did the storekeepers in town, who said they couldn't make any money. And they were all mad at President Hoover because they thought the Depression was his fault.

Mama sighed. "I wish I could teach again, Frank. But the schools don't take married women, and today I'd have to have a certificate from a teacher's college."

"Now don't fret, Lucy. With your nice smile, any store downtown would be happy to take you on as a clerk." Daddy sighed. "Wish I had some o' your book learnin'. It would come in mighty handy about now. But my pa thought all I needed to know was farmin' and didn't send me to school the way he should have."

"Listen to this, Frank." Mama read to him from the front page of the paper. "One fourth of the population in the United States is now out of work."

"Whew!" said Daddy. "Well, Lucy, I don't care what they say. I don't intend to be out o' work very long."

Sarah listened at the sink, ignoring the water that ran down the sides of her glass, wetting her hand. She couldn't wait for Mama and Daddy to get jobs so they could have a house with hot and cold running water and a bathroom with a flush toilet in it. And at least two bedrooms.

Later they all went to bed. The house was quiet but Sarah lay wide awake. She got up and pulled a chain that hung from the ceiling. Watching the light bulb glow, Sarah almost forgot what the rest of the place was like. With electricity there would be no more oil lamps to fill, glass chimneys to wash, and wicks to trim. She turned the light off and on again. Then she froze. She was sure she saw a gray shadow streak across the floor. An animal? She turned the light off and listened. She heard a rustling sound and pulled the chain again. There it was — a rat! It scurried under the cookstove. The light fell across holes in the wall where plaster had fallen.

Sarah threw herself down on her cot and wept. Even with electricity and running water, this was a horrible place. But Daddy had said they wouldn't be here long. On Monday, when he found a job, they'd be out of here lickety-split. If Mama found work too, they might have enough money for new clothes and a movie at the Aladdin Theater once in a while. And they could buy ice cream at the drug-store.

Sarah wondered if there were any nice kids in this neighborhood. She hadn't liked the ones she saw. But it didn't matter, since they'd be moving in a few days anyway. Besides, she was starting at her new school on Monday, only two days from now. She'd always liked school. She couldn't wait to make new friends there and visit them at their houses. Maybe she'd find a friend who liked to bake, and they could make cookies and rolls together, and be best friends. With these thoughts spinning in her head, Sarah fell asleep.

2

chapter

SARAH'S FACE GREW hot as she sat at her desk and listened to the teacher.

"We have a new student in class today," said Miss Macmillan. "Her name is Sarah Ann Puckett." How, Sarah wondered, did the teacher know her middle name? She never went by Sarah Ann, and she had been careful not to mention it. Then she remembered. Her school records had followed her here! Now everyone would know that her initials spelled SAP. To make things even worse, Miss Macmillan wrote Sarah's whole name on the blackboard.

"Sarah Ann," said Miss Macmillan, "stand up so we can all see you."

Sarah wanted to shrink like Alice in Wonderland so she could crawl into the inkwell on her desk and hide there. She rose and sat so quickly that the teacher asked her to stand again.

"Now turn around, Sarah Ann. We want everyone to know who you are." Miss Macmillan smiled at her. Sarah heard a few giggles float across the room as she twirled and sat down. She must look funny, she thought. She hated the patched and faded dress she was wearing. And her shoes, even with new laces and a fresh coat of polish, curled up at the toes and were badly scuffed. Some of the others in the class weren't so well dressed either, but she was sure her clothes were the shabbiest.

Sarah had counted twenty-four kids in this class, some with new shoes and store-bought clothes. And all in sixth grade! At her country school there had been only a dozen in all eight grades, with two in sixth: she and Aline Weber. She'd always been better at her lessons than Aline. She hoped she wouldn't be too far behind this class.

Miss Macmillan picked up a stack of papers from her desk and gave several sheets to each of the kids sitting in front. "Take one and pass them back," she said. Then she stopped and looked at Sarah, who sat near the middle of the room. "You don't have to take this test today if you don't want to."

Curious, Sarah took one of the Ditto sheets with faded purple typing on it and read the ten math story problems. They looked easy and fun to do. Taking a pencil from the groove on her desktop, she quickly did them all. When she finished, everyone else was still working. Then a dark-haired girl in the front row put down her pencil.

"When you've finished, bring your tests to me," said Miss Macmillan. Sarah and the dark-haired girl handed in their papers at the same time. Soon others brought theirs. Miss Macmillan assigned a geography lesson for the class to study while she graded the tests.

A little later the teacher got up from her desk and started writing on the blackboard. Sarah couldn't believe her eyes. Why in the world was she writing Sarah Ann Puckett on the board again? Once was bad enough. Miss Macmillan put a number beside Sarah's name: 100. Then she wrote the name Carla Peterson and put 100 beside it, too. These must be the test grades, thought Sarah. She smiled. Good to know she wasn't behind. The teacher wrote a 90 beside a boy's name and turned toward the class.

"I've written the three highest math scores on the board. Congratulations, particularly to Sarah Ann Puckett. It seems that a very good student has joined our class." Sarah Ann again! Miss Macmillan flashed her a big smile and handed back the top three papers first, then the others. The dark-haired girl must be Carla Peterson, thought Sarah. Pretty girl. Her starched blue dress looked new.

At recess Sarah leaned against the school building and watched as other kids laughed and talked and tossed balls. No one asked her to join in. Breathing in the cool spring air, she thought about her parents. They had both gone out job hunting this morning. She hoped they had found good ones.

On the sidewalk nearby, Carla Peterson played jacks with another nicely dressed girl, and never once looked up at her. In class Sarah had sensed all eyes on her. Now she felt invisible. She didn't know which was worse. She had looked forward to going to a big school in town, but now she could tell it wouldn't be much fun. With only six weeks of school left, she wouldn't have time to make any friends.

As these thoughts trudged through her mind, two girls walked up to her. One was short and blond, the other taller, with brown hair.

"Hello," said the blond girl in a high-pitched voice. "I hear your name is Sarah Ann Puckett."

"Just Sarah. I don't use the Ann."

"I think Sarah Ann suits you," said the girl with brown hair.

"What are your names?" asked Sarah.

The blond girl raised one shoulder as she spoke. "Edna Botts. And this here is Mildred Hotchkiss."

Sarah smiled. "Hi." It was nice of them to come up and speak to her, she thought.

Mildred giggled. "Did you know that your initials spell SAP?"

"Yes," said Sarah. "I hear that if your initials spell a word, it means you're going to be rich someday."

"You sure don't look rich now," said Edna. "Where'd you get that dress?"

"And those shoes?" Mildred chimed in.

So they were going to be nasty, were they? Rather than answer their questions, Sarah asked them one. "Do your initials spell anything?"

"Not mine," said Mildred.

"Mine neither." Edna raised her shoulder again. "Your last name rhymes with bucket. Did you know that? Bein' from a farm, you oughta know what a bucket is."

Anger churned inside Sarah. She walked away from them and again leaned against the building. Out of the corner of her eye she saw the two girls whispering. There must be some nice kids in this school, thought Sarah, but she hadn't met them yet. Maybe she never would.

Soon a boy joined Edna and Mildred, and the three

stared at Sarah and laughed. The boy looked familiar. With those close-set eyes and thick nose, he had to be a brother to the two who had ridden their running board on moving day. Miss Macmillan had called him Jake Scully and scolded him in class. He looked older than the other sixth-graders. He'd probably been held back because he flunked, thought Sarah.

When the three of them walked up to her, Sarah decided not to move. Her knees were shaking but she wasn't going to let on that she was scared.

"Think you're smart, doncha?" said Jake.

They were ganging up on her. So this was what town school was like! "I'm not as dumb as some people," she said.

"Listen to her," said Mildred. "Her head's all swelled up just 'cause she got that hundred. Hearin' her talk so big and stuck up, you'd think she was some doctor's kid like Carla Peterson."

"She ain't no doctor's kid," said Edna. "Look at them clothes. Straight off the farm."

Anger and fear fought inside Sarah. "If all town kids are like you three, I'll take the farm any day." Her brave words came out in a trembly voice.

"Listen to that," said Jake. "That fast mouth's gonna get you in trouble."

"She's a sap," said Edna. "And her last name rhymes with bucket. Yeah!" She raised her shoulder. "Sap bucket! That's what she is. A sap bucket!"

Jake Scully hawked and spit on the sidewalk. "She looks more like a slop bucket to me."

16

Mildred shrieked with laughter. "Slop bucket!"

"Slop bucket," echoed Edna. "That's a scream!"

Furious, Sarah gritted her teeth. She wondered what Mama and Daddy would say when she told them about these three.

On her way home from school that day, Sarah had stopped at Mr. Neely's store to pick up some groceries for Mama. Carrying her sack across the railroad tracks, she saw a bunch of kids—about seven or eight—milling around on the front porch with the broken railing. Jake Scully was among them, with his thick-nosed brother and sister. They all wore ragged clothes, and several looked like the ones Mama and Daddy had kicked out of their house on moving day. Sarah would have turned and walked in another direction, but she didn't know any other way to get home. Instead, she cut across the street, walking faster and gripping her sack with damp hands. Jake crossed too, and followed her.

"Hey, come on!" he yelled. "Slop Bucket has some eats!" The others ran across and made a tight circle around Sarah, forcing her to stop.

"Whatcha got in that sack?" asked one.

"None of your business." Her voice shook.

"She ain't a bit friendly," said Jake's sister. Then her brother, the boy who had ridden on their truck and sassed Mama, reached into Sarah's bag and pulled out a big potato. He yelled a swear word and tossed the potato on the ground.

"Who needs a potato? Where are the cookies?"

A bigger boy and another girl grabbed the sack out of Sarah's arms and turned it over on the sidewalk. "Let's find the goodies," said the girl. But when only potatoes, flour, yeast, and a can of peas spilled out onto the cracked and weedy pavement, the whole group yelled and swore.

"Not even any bread," muttered one. "C'mon. She's a waste of time." They all crossed the street and scattered. Sarah put the groceries back into her sack and hurried home. Angry tears streamed down her face.

Mama was home, sweeping the kitchen floor, when Sarah walked in. "What's wrong, dear?" she asked. Sarah told her all that had happened on the playground and on the way home.

"This has to stop," cried Mama. "When your father hears about it, he'll be furious."

"Did you get a job, Mama?" Sarah asked.

"No, dear. But I'll try again tomorrow. The stores aren't taking on any new clerks right now. There was a dentist who needed a secretary. The job would have paid seven dollars a week, but he wanted someone who could type and take shorthand."

Later Daddy came home. "I looked hard all day," he said, "but I didn't find a doggone thing. There must have been fifty people lined up to see about work at the creamery. Then the foreman came out and said they weren't hiring today. Same thing happened at the flour mill, only worse. The boss said they had just laid off several workers and probably wouldn't need any help until business improved."

One more disappointment, thought Sarah. It had been an awful day. She had so hoped that Daddy would have good news for them, and that they'd start looking for a better house right away.

Mama sighed and told Daddy that she hadn't found work either. "Well, Frank, tomorrow's another day."

Sarah told Daddy about the mean kids. Mama suggested that both she and Daddy talk to their parents or teachers. Daddy studied his hands in silence, then looked at Mama. "Talkin' to the parents or teachers might make things worse for Sarah. I remember how it was when I was growin' up. Kids hate tattlers."

"Well, how about giving me a ride to school and back?" Sarah asked.

"Can't afford it right now, Sarah. I have to save the gas for job huntin'. Besides, when I start workin' I won't have time to drive you back and forth."

Sarah felt the tears rise in her throat. She missed their dog Leo. If they had kept him, he could have walked to school with her and she could have trained him to meet her and walk home with her. He was a big dog, part chow and part collie. He wouldn't have let those nasty kids come near her. But Mama and Daddy said they couldn't afford to keep him in town and gave him to Mr. Miller.

"When you're dealin' with toughs," said Daddy, "you have to fight back. I've always said that if you look under a bully's hide, you'll more'n likely find a coward."

"Daddy's right," said Mama. "You must stand up to them."

"You can do it, Sarah," said Daddy. "You're big for your age and plenty strong. I'll bet you could hold your own real well."

"But, Daddy, there are so many of them. And I don't know anything about fighting."

"It's time you learned," he said. "Come here. I'm gonna teach you a few tricks." He got up from his chair and gripped her wrist tightly with his hand. "Know what to do when somebody holds you like this?"

Sarah shook her head. "No, what?"

Daddy showed her how to free herself by thrusting her wrist against his thumb.

"It works, Daddy! It works!" Sarah couldn't believe how easy it was.

"I'll teach you some other tricks, too," said Daddy. "You oughta learn how to trip kids while they walk, and how to punch 'em in the nose or jaw. And how to kick where it hurts. 'Course you'll have to train some. But after a week or two you should be ready."

Sarah wasn't sure she'd ever be able to lick the tough neighborhood kids, no matter how many lessons she had. But since Daddy was offering to train her, she wasn't going to turn him down.

3

---

c h a p t e r

O N A SATURDAY morning nearly three weeks later, Sarah sat beside Daddy on the riverbank. They each held a fishing rod, waiting for a bite.

"Have you faced up to the bullies yet?" asked Daddy.

"Not yet," said Sarah. "Maybe I need more fighting lessons." The late April sun warmed her back as she watched the trees' wavy reflection in the water. She was scared to fight, but didn't want Daddy to know that she was such a coward.

"I've taught you every trick in my book," her father said. "You're mighty nimble and quick, and a fast learner, too. Are the kids at school still pickin' on you?"

Sarah nodded. Almost every day those three nasty kids followed her on the school grounds, threatening her and calling her Slop Bucket. On the way to and from school, the gang down the street, the bunch who had dumped her groceries, still bothered her. Once they'd snatched her lunch bag. Another time they ran off with her notebook and scattered her school papers all over the street. Fighting them would be like taking on a whole army. She often took the long way to school, through backyards and alleyways,

21

detouring around the Scully house, which seemed to be the gang's headquarters.

"Been makin' any new friends?" Daddy asked.

"No." Sarah stared at the flowing river water, thick with mud. She had never felt so lonely in her life. With no friends, she found herself missing the farm animals more than she thought she would. Especially Leo, and the calf she had been raising for the fair. And their cows and two horses, and the kittens and cats that lived in their barn. On the farm, with no other kids around, the animals had been good company. At school, everyone in her class ignored her. Looked right through her, as if she was invisible. Only three weeks of school left until summer vacation, thank goodness.

"Daddy, can't we move to a better part of town?" she asked. They had hoped to be out of Shantytown by now.

He sighed. "Not till I find steady work. We've looked. Rent's too high anywhere else."

It was taking Daddy forever to find a job, thought Sarah. He had done a few days' work for the city, digging ditches for water and sewer lines, but when the job was finished he was out of work again. At least he'd earned five dollars, which helped.

Mama hadn't found a job either. All the business owners in town told her they were too broke to hire anyone. So she had stopped looking two weeks ago and swapped the dining room furniture for a used washing machine. The minister at their church had talked some folks into bringing Mama their washing and ironing.

Life in town wasn't what Sarah had hoped for. So far

she hadn't set foot inside the Aladdin Theater, nor had she bought candy or eaten ice cream at the drugstore. In fact, she felt lucky to eat anything at all. She hoped one of them would catch a fish pretty soon. They'd been sitting out there a long time. Whenever Daddy was able to shoot a rabbit or a squirrel they had meat for dinner. Sarah liked rabbit, but she thought squirrel's dark meat tasted too gamey.

A splashing sound roused Sarah from her thoughts. Daddy was lifting his bent rod, reeling in something dark and heavy. It flopped and wriggled. "Hey, look at that!" he cried. "A dandy catfish. We eat."

As they walked toward home, the late morning sun shone through the budding branches. Sarah breathed in the grassy scent of spring and glanced down at the catfish. It would be delicious when Mama rolled it in cornmeal and fried it. She thought about the bread dough she had left to rise in the kitchen. It would be ready to bake when they got back. She always looked forward to bread making.

When Sarah and Daddy walked in the door, Mama was bent over the ironing board, pressing pleats in a beautiful red print dress. Sarah wished it were hers, but until Daddy found steady work she could only dream about owning such fancy things. Her mother's hard work, even with the washing machine, didn't bring in enough money to pay their bills. She'd heard Mama and Daddy talk about it. Scary talk.

Heaping boxes of clothes filled the tiny house. Every chair was piled high. Mama had strung wires across the ceiling in the kitchen for hanging up freshly ironed shirts and dresses. The house always smelled of lye soap and boiling starch.

"I see you brought us a fish," said Mama. She wiped her brow. Sarah noticed that her mother didn't smile as much as she used to. Mama licked her finger and touched the bottom of the heavy flatiron to test its warmth. Then she picked up a smaller one and placed it on the cookstove to heat.

Daddy held up the fish. "I'll go outside and clean this."

"Good," said Mama. "I'll be ready to fry it as soon as I finish with this dress. Sarah, your bread looks ready to bake. You might want to put it in the oven now."

After a delicious catfish dinner that noon, Daddy left the house to look for work. Sarah was pulling her fresh loaves from the oven when a Mrs. Tilden stopped by to pick up her laundry from Mama. She was a jolly woman whose double chins wobbled as she talked.

"My, what a wonderful smell!" She watched Sarah turn her loaves out onto a cooling rack. "Did you bake all those yourself?"

"Yes," said Sarah. "Baking's my hobby."

"Sarah's bread won first prize at the county fair last fall." Mama smiled at Sarah. "She's our blue-ribbon champion and does all our baking now."

"You don't say!" exclaimed Mrs. Tilden. "You wouldn't consider selling a loaf to me now and then, would you? I just love homemade bread, but I don't bake very often."

Sarah grinned. "Sure I'll sell you a loaf." How wonderful

it would be, she thought, to have some money of her own. She looked first at her mother, then at Mrs. Tilden.

"What do you charge?" the woman asked.

Sarah hesitated before saying fifteen cents. She knew it was more than the dime the grocery store got for bread. But hers was special and fresh.

Mrs. Tilden twisted the fastener on her leather coin purse and handed Sarah the money. "There you are," she said. "I hope you'll have another one ready for me when I come back next Saturday."

"Thanks. I will." Sarah handed her a warm loaf.

After Mrs. Tilden left, Sarah watched Mama put her laundry money, several coins, into the cracked sugar bowl on the windowsill. Sarah stared at the dime and nickel in the palm of her hand. Should she keep it for herself or give it to Mama for groceries? She knew that her parents needed every penny. But what if Daddy came home this evening with a job? They wouldn't need it then. If she gave it to Mama now, it would be rude to ask her to give it back. She'd wait.

Fifteen cents! It was too good to be true. It would buy three ice cream cones or one chocolate soda and a nickel sack of candy. If she saved it and put it with next week's money, she could go to a movie and have an ice cream cone afterward. The only thing she didn't like about being twelve was that she could no longer get into the picture show for a dime. It would cost her a quarter. She looked up and saw Mama smiling at her.

"Mama, she paid me fifteen cents! And she wants an-other loaf next week."

"I know. What are you going to do with all that money?"

"I haven't decided yet. I'll have to think about it." Sarah reached under her cot, pulled out her lucky box, and placed the dime and nickel beside her shiny blue ribbon. The day had been a good one, but it would be absolutely perfect if Daddy found a steady job.

Her father came home at sundown. Looking tired and disappointed, he slumped into a chair. He had found no job.

"Did you go to the auto repair shop?" asked Mama.

"Yep. The foreman said they're turning down thirty or forty people every day. Seems I'm not alone."

"But, Frank!" Mama cried. "You're a wonderful mechanic. You know all about engines and cars and tractors."

Daddy sighed. "Nobody gives a hoot about what you're able to do, or how hard you're willing to work. It's the Depression, Lucy. These are terrible times. There aren't any jobs because business is bad. And business is bad because people without jobs can't buy anything. Now give me the answer to that one!"

During supper sadness hung in the air, and nobody talked much. On top of everything else, thought Sarah, the evening meal hadn't been very good. Rice and lima beans. The catfish they'd had at noon was all gone, and several days ago they'd eaten the last jars of home-canned tomatoes and green beans from the farm.

Daddy spoke at last. "Tomorrow I'll give the feed store another try. Last week they said one of their helpers might be movin' outa town."

26

Mama smiled at him. "Frank, I've had this feeling all along that the feed store would be the perfect place for you. You know all about the different types of poultry feed. And they handle seeds, too. With all your farming experience, there isn't anything you don't know about seeds. Who could be better qualified than you?"

Daddy swallowed and stroked his coffee cup. "Don't get your hopes up, Lucy. If there's any chance at all, it'll be a slim one." From the shadowy look on his face, Sarah could tell that her father was worried.

After supper Sarah opened her good luck box and removed the nickel and dime. With all the trouble her parents were having, she felt guilty about keeping the money. After all, her mother had bought the flour and yeast she had used to make the bread. Mama stood at the table, sprinkling a pile of shirts for the next day's ironing. Sarah walked over to her and held out the fifteen cents.

"What's that for?" Mama asked.

"Groceries."

Mama hugged her. "You're a good girl, Sarah. But I hate to take your money."

"It's all right," Sarah said. "Here." She laid it on the table.

Mama smiled at her and picked it up. Then she handed the dime back to Sarah. "I won't take all of it. You need some money of your own. I'll just take enough to pay for the flour and yeast you used. After all, you made that loaf yourself and were clever enough to sell it for a good price."

Sarah was thrilled. She had a whole dime to keep. Mama was being very fair, she thought. She wondered if more of

27

her mother's customers would buy her bread. Maybe she should make an extra batch next Saturday just to sell. She checked their flour and yeast supply. There was barely enough for next week's six loaves.

"Mama," she said, "if I bake an extra batch of bread next Saturday, I bet I could sell it."

Mama looked up from the shirts. "You have a good idea there, Sarah."

"But we don't have enough flour and yeast. When you go to the store, buy some extra, will you?"

"We'll see," said Mama.

Sarah knew why Mama wasn't promising anything. They probably couldn't afford extra flour and yeast. At least not until Daddy got a job.

Later that night, as Sarah lay awake in her cot, she heard Mama and Daddy talking in their room.

"Lucy," said Daddy, "I saw an awful thing today. After I left the repair shop, I was walkin' down the alley behind the Meadowlark café. One o' the cooks came out the back door with a bucket o' garbage. You know, bones and scraps from people's plates. Well, he set it down on the ground and left it. There musta been five men waitin' there, grabbin' and fightin' over that food like a bunch o' dogs."

"These are hard times all right," said Mama.

"Hard's not the word for it," said Daddy. "These are desperate times. People are starvin', Lucy."

Sarah closed her eyes and tried to erase the scene Daddy had described, but it wouldn't go away.

4

c h a p t e r

O<small>N MONDAY MORNING</small> Sarah leaned against the school building, waiting for the bell. She felt alone and miserable, but at least those three mean kids hadn't noticed her yet.

The sun hid behind a cloud. Suddenly cool, Sarah shivered and hoped it wouldn't rain. During a storm last week, rain had leaked through their roof in the middle of the night. She'd had to move her cot to stay dry. The next morning Mama hadn't been able to hang out her wash.

Clutching her schoolbooks close to her chest, Sarah thought about Daddy. She crossed her fingers for luck, and made a wish that he'd find a job that day.

Sarah felt the coin in her jacket pocket. She'd brought her dime with her, and planned to spend some of it that afternoon on her way home from school. Maybe all of it. For ice cream.

Sarah was jolted from her thoughts by familiar loud voices.

"Four Eyes! Four Eyes! Ha ha ha!" The mean kids. But the words were different this time, and Sarah wondered who was getting it. She spotted them by the swings: Edna Botts, Mildred Hotchkiss, and Jake Scully. They were teasing Carla Peterson. She couldn't believe it. Carla! One of the smartest and best-liked girls in their class. Curious, Sarah stepped closer. She noticed that Carla was wearing eyeglasses for the first time, and that her face had turned red. She knew how Carla felt.

Edna raised her shoulder in that stuck-up way she had. "That's what you get for all that studying! You could go blind if you don't watch out."

"Yeah," said Mildred in her shrill voice. "With her nose in a book all the time, she needs four eyes."

"Her nose ain't in a book all the time," said Edna. "Sometimes she sticks it in the air."

"Why don't you hang specs around your neck, too?" yelled Jake. "Good to have a spare in case somebody socks you in the face." Carla turned and walked away from them, but they followed her.

If there was ever a chance to get even with those three, thought Sarah, it was now, while they were busy with Carla. It was a made-to-order situation. According to Daddy, it was always best to take the enemy by surprise. She was scared, but she wanted to try it. Even if she lost, they probably wouldn't kill her. If she didn't do it, she'd always think of herself as a coward.

She set her books on the ground, and walked along behind them. So far so good. Nobody had noticed her. Trying hard to remember her father's lessons, she sneaked up behind Edna. Sarah quickly placed her foot between Edna's feet and tripped her. At the same time she pushed Mildred from behind, hard. Both girls fell forward, yelling.

Sarah whirled around to run, but Jake Scully darted in front of her and grabbed her wrists. Sarah unlocked his grasp by thrusting her wrists against his thumbs. Jake must have been surprised, because his mouth flew open. Sarah then made a fist and socked him in the jaw. His mouth snapped shut from the blow, his upper teeth biting into his lower lip. Sarah turned and walked away, leaving the two girls to nurse their scrapes and Jake to wipe the blood off his chin. Inside she glowed. She had done it. Daddy would be proud. She'd taken on the three of them and won.

In the speed of the fight, Sarah had forgotten about Carla. Then she heard a voice behind her.

"Hey, wait!"

Sarah stopped and turned around.

Carla caught up, her dark hair flying in the wind. "Where'd you learn to fight like that?"

"My daddy taught me some things. Why?"

"Thanks." Carla's new glasses slid down the bridge of her nose. She pushed them back with her finger.

"I did it for all the times they called me Slop Bucket," said Sarah.

"Slop Bucket? You're kidding!" Carla threw back her head and exploded into laughter. The joyful sound of it made Sarah laugh too.

"Know what?" Carla's eyes crinkled at the corners. "Those dummies have bothered me ever since second grade."

Sarah couldn't believe what she'd just heard. Carla Peterson? Pretty, bright, well-dressed Carla Peterson? The girl who had everything?

"Why would they pick on you?" she asked.

"Can't you guess? The same reason they pester you."

31

Sarah stared at Carla's starched pink dress with matching sweater.

"But they tease me about my clothes," said Sarah. "Your clothes are beautiful."

Carla smiled. "Aw, that's not the real reason. They just say those things to get your goat. What they really hate is your brains. They can't stand it because you're smart and they're stupid."

So Carla had noticed her after all! Sarah smiled and held out her hand. "Meet Slop Bucket, Four Eyes."

Carla shook her hand and the two girls giggled. The bell rang and they slowly walked toward the building together. "I want to ask you something," Carla said. "How do I really look in my glasses? I want the truth."

Sarah studied Carla's face. She saw a pretty girl with warm brown eyes and pink cheeks. "Pretty," she said. "And a little studious maybe."

"Thanks. For the pretty part, I mean. And you're probably right about the studious. I like to read. Do you?"

"Sure," said Sarah. "But I don't have many books."

"You'll have to go to the library. You can borrow all kinds of books there. And it's free."

Sarah had heard about Waheegan's public library. "I'd like to go there," she said. "Where is it?"

But Carla had stopped talking. Sarah looked up to see Miss Macmillan facing them.

"Sarah Ann Puckett!" the teacher cried. "Several people have told me that you've been fighting on the school grounds. Is that true?"

Sarah swallowed and felt herself blush. "Yes ma'am. I guess it is."

"Why, Sarah Ann, I'm ashamed of you," she said. "I'll have to keep you in at recess. And you'll be staying after school too."

What rotten luck, thought Sarah. Just when she was getting to know one of the nice kids.

After school Sarah refused to answer Miss Macmillan's questions about why she had fought. Tattling would just make things worse. For being what her teacher called stubborn, Sarah had to stay another five minutes and listen to Miss Macmillan lecture her about how wicked it was to fight. Sarah wondered if Miss Macmillan had ever been called Slop Bucket or Four Eyes. She guessed not.

As Sarah left the quiet building, she saw Carla sitting on the steps, reading. The sun had come out and was shining on her dark hair, bringing out its reddish highlights. She stood up. "I waited for you. I can walk with you as far as my house. I've seen you go by."

Sarah couldn't believe her ears. Was Carla Peterson actually offering to walk with her? And she had waited ten whole minutes. "Sure. It was nice of you to wait."

"Did you tell Miss Macmillan why you fought?" asked Carla.

"No."

"Why not?"

"Aw, I didn't want to squeal." Sarah wondered if Carla would care to be seen with her when other kids were around. If only she had some decent clothes.

"Was Miss Macmillan mad when you didn't explain?"

"Yeah. She said I was stubborn and made me stay five minutes longer."

Carla smiled. "Really? I can't believe you wouldn't tell. That's great."

"Did they bother you anymore?" Sarah asked.

"The three dummies? No. I think you've stopped them."

Sarah was pleased. "What did you do at recess?"

"Played hopscotch and catch. Maybe you can play with us tomorrow."

Was Carla really asking her to join in games with her friends? It seemed too good to be true. She hoped Carla wouldn't forget when tomorrow came.

As the two girls walked along, they talked about how neither of them had brothers or sisters and wished they had. They found a lot to laugh about. Carla saw the funny side of everything and made Sarah see it too. They hooted over the way Miss Macmillan always flared her nostrils before she bawled you out. And the way Edna Botts raised her shoulder when she was being nasty. And how the Scully girl, who was in the class behind them, surely combed her hair with an eggbeater and never washed her face. By the time they reached Carla's house, they were giggling at the least little thing until their ribs ached.

Sarah looked up at Carla's two-story home. It was pretty; shiny white, with window shutters and a front door painted dark green. She didn't want to say good-bye to

Carla just as they were starting to get acquainted. She felt the dime in her pocket and had an idea.

"Want to go downtown with me and get an ice cream cone?" asked Sarah. "I have money."

"Sure," said Carla. "Come on in. I'll ask my mother."

Inside Carla's house, Sarah walked softly, as if afraid of trampling its beauty. The polished tables shone, and so did the plump chairs covered in satin. Sarah admired the starched lace doilies under the table lamps. Her feet sank into the thick rug as she followed Carla to the back of the house. In the gleaming kitchen, Carla introduced Sarah to her mother. Sarah stared in wonder at the electric refrigerator. Its round motor on top was like a humming white cage. And the stove had gas burners. Everything was so modern. The smell of roasting meat was making Sarah hungry. She couldn't wait to eat that ice cream cone.

"You may go," said Carla's mother. "But please be back here in half an hour, to practice."

"I will." Carla explained to Sarah that she took piano lessons. The two girls dashed out the door.

At the drugstore Sarah and Carla sat on wire-backed chairs pulled up to a tiny round table. They each licked an ice cream cone and giggled. When they finished the two girls walked out of the drugstore arm in arm.

"Thanks for the cone," said Carla. "Can you come over to my house after school tomorrow? I'll show you my room."

"I think I can. I'll ask."

"And stop by my house in the morning, so we can walk together."

"Sure." When they parted, Sarah ran home. She was brimming over with news to tell Mama and Daddy. About the fight, and Carla. I've made a friend, she thought, I've made a friend! She flew past the Scully house, feeling lucky that the gang was nowhere in sight. When she reached home she burst into the kitchen.

"Mama!" she cried. "Carla Peterson has invited me to her house tomorrow. She's this really nice girl I met at school. May I go?"

Her mother looked up at her from the ironing board. She was crying, and wiped away the tears with the back of her hand. "I think so," she said.

"Mama, what's wrong?"

"I'd rather not talk about it. You may find out soon enough. Please help me hang out some clothes now."

"Sure, Mama." Concern for her mother dampened the gaiety Sarah had felt.

As they hung the clothes Mama kept sniffling and blinking her eyes.

"What is it, Mama? Tell me."

"It's Daddy. Something he said at dinner this noon, while you were at school." Just then Sarah heard the truck turn into the yard and stop in front of the house.

"Shhh! He's here," Mama whispered. "We can't talk about it now."

Sarah swallowed hard. What did "it" mean? What was going on? She thrust her cold hands into her empty jacket pockets and studied Daddy as he walked toward the house.

5

chapter

BEFORE HER FATHER reached the door, Sarah ran to him and told him about the fight at school and how she had made a new friend.

"That's my girl." He grinned at her and patted her shoulder. "You took on all three of 'em?"

She nodded. "Uh-huh."

"I'll be doggoned. You're a real champ! But o' course I knew it all the time."

Sarah studied his face. He certainly seemed normal enough. What had Mama been so upset about?

At supper that evening Sarah kept waiting for "it" to be mentioned. Soon after Daddy came in he'd told them that he hadn't found a job yet. But so far at least, that had never been enough to send Mama into a crying fit for half a day. Mama passed the lima beans to Sarah and Daddy in silence. Then the rice. The amount was so small that Sarah had to be careful to leave enough for Daddy and Mama. For the past three days, lima beans and rice or potatoes was all they'd had to eat at supper. And there wasn't really enough for three people. Mornings they had a small dab of oatmeal.

Sarah couldn't help thinking about how much food

they'd always had on the farm, and how good it had been. They'd had ham and eggs and meat every day. Butter, too, and milk from their own cows. But here in town they ate their bread dry, and all Sarah had to drink was water. The coffee was all used up, and Mama only rarely made tea for herself and Daddy from a package she had saved from the farm. When they'd lived in the country, although Daddy often talked about debts and crop failure, they always had plenty to eat.

"Mama, can't you afford to go to the grocery store?" asked Sarah.

Her mother looked at her with reddened eyes. "No, dear. We'll just have to eat what we have on hand. When the weather turns warmer, we can plant a few vegetables next to the house, and eat the mulberries from the tree. If we're lucky we can catch a fish now and then, or shoot a rabbit or a squirrel."

Sarah stared at her plate. She thought about the ice cream she'd had with Carla that afternoon. Too bad Mama and Daddy didn't get any. If she could sell lots of bread, she might bring home some nicer food from the grocery store, like cookies or hamburger. Or she might even buy a whole pint of ice cream to have for dessert sometime. "Mama," she said, "I'm going to need some extra flour, for selling bread."

"I know, dear," said her mother. "But we can't buy it now. I'm saving every penny to pay the rent and the electric bill."

"I can sell a loaf to Mrs. Tilden, can't I?"

Mama's brows came together. "I suppose, since you've promised her. That is, if she still wants one."

"She will." Sarah was thinking hard. Surely Daddy would have a job in a week or two. But if he didn't, she might have to figure out a way to buy the flour and yeast herself.

She glanced across the table. Her father was looking down at his plate. His hand trembled when he reached for his water glass.

"How did it go today, Frank?" asked Mama.

Daddy sighed. "Same story. I'd rather not talk about it, I guess."

"Were any new buildings going up?" asked Mama.

"Yep," he said. "There were two, but neither of 'em needed a hand."

Mama took a sip of water. "How about the creamery and the ice plant?"

Daddy speared a bean with his fork. "Nothing's changed, Lucy. They were firin', not hirin'."

Mama bit her lip. "Did you go back to the brick plant and the feed mill?"

"Yes, Lucy, I did. And there were no jobs. After a while I walked by some yards where the grass needed cuttin', and knocked on doors. But the folks I talked to figured on mowin' their own lawns." Daddy sighed again and cleaned his plate.

Sarah had an idea. "There's an empty building downtown, Daddy. It's right across from Neely's Variety. Why don't you start a store there?"

39

"You've forgotten something, Sarah," said Daddy. "It takes heaps o' money to start a store. And money is mighty scarce around here."

"Something will turn up," said Mama. "I know it will."

Daddy put down his fork. "Then you know a lot more about it than I do, Lucy. I've even thought about selling brushes or spices door to door, but I don't have the money to get started, or the clothes. I'd need a new suit. I think the only answer is what we talked about this noon."

"No, Frank! I won't hear of it! Please don't mention it again." Mama's eyes filled with tears.

Sarah sat up straight and waited. Here was the subject that had upset Mama so much.

"It's the only thing that makes sense," said Daddy. "I hear that farther out West, in Colorado and California, the Depression hasn't hit as hard. I could ride the rails and get off at the stops to look for work. Then when I get some money ahead, I'll send you some. And when I work into somethin' steady, the two of you can come to wherever I am, and we can live together again."

Sarah gasped. Surely Daddy couldn't mean what he was saying!

Mama took his hand. Her voice shook as she said, "Frank, it's too dangerous to ride the rails. I won't have it. What if you got hurt or sick? Some of those men who ride boxcars are mean and tough. You could be murdered in your sleep by some drunken hobo and we'd never know what happened to you."

"Now don't you worry, Lucy," said Daddy. "I'll be all

40

right. I know how to take care of myself. Besides, I don't think we have any choice. The way things are going here in Waheegan, we'll slowly starve to death."

"We're still eating," said Mama.

"But for how long?" asked Daddy. "We can't go on like this. We just can't. Besides, I feel like a heel eating up your share of the food."

"I know you won't like what I'm about to say, Frank," said Mama, "but we could apply to the county for relief. It would help to tide us over until you find a job."

"Well, Lucy, I swallowed my pride and went to the county office this afternoon."

"What did they say, Frank?"

"The relief funds are all used up. The treasury's broke. No more money for the poor until next year, and maybe none then."

Mama swallowed and studied Daddy's face. "We could write to Alice and Sam," she said. "I'm sure they'd be glad to help us out."

"No, Lucy," said Daddy. "I don't want to go cryin' to your sister in Iowa or anyone else. Besides, I'll bet Alice and Sam haven't a spare nickel to their names. When you write to 'em, please don't let on about our trouble."

Sarah watched Mama cry and felt as if the Depression was circling above their house like a giant hawk, ready to swoop down and snatch Daddy away from them.

Her father got up from the table, went over to where Mama sat, and patted her shoulder. "You've got your laundry business. And since school will soon be out for the

41

summer, Sarah will have more time to lend you a hand. The way it is, I'm just a big worry and another mouth to feed."

Stunned, Sarah grabbed Daddy around his waist. "Don't go, Daddy, please! Mama and I need you."

"Now don't you start in too," he said. "It won't be forever. Just long enough to get a start somewhere else. And I'd better do it during the summer. If I wait until cold weather sets in, it'll be too late."

They had to make him change his mind, thought Sarah. Without Daddy to comfort them, life in this town of strangers, and in this scary neighborhood, would be too awful to imagine.

Mama stood up and faced him. "I won't have it, Frank! You're talking nonsense. The Depression is all over the country. You can't run away from it. Promise me that you will never mention this crazy idea again. Ever."

Daddy studied her face and sighed. "All right, Lucy. I promise I won't say another word about it, but every day I hang around here idle, I feel like a worthless bum."

"A fine man like you won't be idle long," said Mama. "You'll see that I'm right. And you're certainly no bum."

"Thanks." He tilted up her chin, smiled at her, and kissed her gently. But when he held her close and looked over her shoulder, Sarah noticed that his face turned sober. It was as if he were saying one thing and thinking another.

6

c h a p t e r

"Bye!"

"See ya!"

Sarah ran down the steps of Carla Peterson's house. That afternoon the two girls had spent an hour giggling, trying to piece together a jigsaw puzzle in Carla's room. If there was one person in the world who could make her forget her troubles, thought Sarah, it was Carla.

Since the start of their friendship two weeks earlier, they had walked to and from school together every day. On the playground Sarah was included in games with Carla and her friends, and Sarah often visited Carla's house after school. That day Mrs. Peterson, as she always did when Sarah came, had given them fresh baked cookies and milk. Sarah looked forward to this delicious treat because food at their house was pretty scarce. Daddy still hadn't found a steady job, though he'd had a few days' work repairing a road west of town. He was pretty discouraged, but he left the house early every morning, hoping to find a real job. At least Daddy no longer talked about going west.

Sarah had waited two weeks for Mama to buy extra flour and yeast, but there hadn't been enough money. For the past two Saturdays she had sold a loaf to Mrs. Tilden, but she wanted to sell more. Out of every fifteen cents she earned, she still gave Mama one nickel, for the flour and yeast. And she had found that ten cents a week didn't go very far, especially when you tried to take home a treat from the grocery store and share your penny candy with a friend. Last Saturday she had brought home several cookies for dessert, something to pep up their meal a little. A whole week's earnings gone in one day. Poof! Just like that. Besides, with only four days of school left, she had to think about summer. She didn't want to spend all her time helping Mama with the laundry.

On her way home Sarah stopped at Neely's grocery store.

"How much is a ten-pound sack of flour?" she asked.

Mr. Neely, a balding man with large ears, leaned across the counter. "Thirty cents."

"And how much is a cake of yeast?"

"Three cents. But I'll let you have ten for a quarter."

Sarah opened her school tablet and jotted the figures down. She was sure she could get twelve loaves out of a thirty-cent sack of flour and nine cents' worth of yeast. If she charged fifteen cents a loaf, she could make a dollar and forty-one cents' profit. But she needed thirty-nine cents right away. If only she'd saved her money instead of spending it on treats! Next Saturday she'd probably get ten cents from the fifteen she charged Mrs. Tilden, but it would take four weeks of saving to have enough. The way things were going at home, Mama might not even have the money to buy flour for their own baking. Unless Daddy got a job right away.

"Mr. Neely," she said, "do you ever sell on credit?"

"Been doin' a lot o' that lately," he said. "What's your name?"

"Puckett. Sarah Puckett."

He looked up something in a thick, clothbound book. "Got a Frank Puckett here. You his daughter?"

"Yes." Sarah thought it strange that her father's name was in a book of Mr. Neely's.

"Afraid your family's used up all the credit they're gonna get." He snapped the book shut. "Until they settle some on their bill, they're gonna have to pay cash."

Sarah was startled. "How much do they owe?" She'd checked their flour and yeast supply at home. Six loaves' worth. Barely enough for themselves and one loaf for Mrs. Tilden.

"My books show about five dollars."

Five dollars! How could they ever pay it? Then there was the electric bill. And the rent on that tacky house they lived in was five dollars a month. She'd heard Mama talk to Daddy about it. Her mother's laundry brought in only three or four dollars a week. Her parents must have known that their credit at the grocery store was gone, but hadn't said anything about it.

Sarah glanced at the dusty cans and packages on the shelves. Some items had been there a long time. Trash had gathered on the floor in the corners. The place needed a good cleaning. Sarah had an idea.

45

"What would you pay," she asked, "if I dusted your shelves and swept? I could wash your windows, too."

"Well," said Mr. Neely, "if you're offerin' to work off some of your family's debt, I might consider it."

"That wasn't what I had in mind," said Sarah. "I need the money."

"Well now, young lady, money's mighty hard to come by these days. 'Fraid I can't pay you in cash."

If he couldn't pay money, she thought, maybe he'd pay in groceries. It was worth a try. "Then how about ten pounds of flour and three cakes of yeast?"

"Flour and yeast, huh? Whatcha gonna do with it?"

"Bake bread," said Sarah. "To sell."

He grinned. "So ya wanta run me out o' the bread business?"

"I could let you buy some from me. To sell in the store."

He laughed. "Quite a business head you got there, kid. Why don't you come in after school tomorrow. I could use somebody to sweep up and wash shelves. With about five hours of good hard work you can have your ten-pound sack o' flour and nine cents' worth o' yeast." Mr. Neely smiled at her.

Sarah's head whirled. "I'll ask my parents." If she worked after school the rest of this week, she wouldn't be able to go to Carla's house. She'd miss the fun, of course, and the cookies and milk. But her friend would surely understand.

"Come here, Sarah." Mr. Neely beckoned her to follow him behind the meat counter. "Want to show you something." At the big cutting table, he picked up a knife and

46

placed his other hand on a huge hunk of beef. "I was goin' to trim this down a little and slice it for the showcase. Always have a few scraps left. If you wanta wait, you can take some home with you."

"Thank you, Mr. Neely. That would be wonderful." For all his gruff manner, he seemed like a nice man.

As she often did on her way home, Sarah stood in front of the vacant store building on Main Street. She stroked the soft meat package Mr. Neely had just given her and studied the sign tucked into the corner of the show window: FOR RENT OR SALE. Printed under those words was the name of the man in charge, a Mr. Willard. From her first day in Waheegan, this building had stirred up dreams in Sarah's head.

She shaded her eyes and pressed her nose against one of the two empty windows. She never saw the rubbish and cobwebs inside. She always pictured Daddy in there, behind the counter of his own store, pushing the buttons on a fancy cash register. Sometimes Mama was in there too, helping him. What kind of store? Some days it was a dress shop, but she really couldn't imagine Daddy selling dresses. Other times it was food. All the things she liked: ice cream, candy, and jams and jellies. Or a shoe shop. She loved new shoes. But Daddy had said he didn't have the money to start a store.

Walking home, Sarah kept an eye out for the neighborhood gang near the Scully house, but saw no one. Her thoughts went back to Mr. Neely's offer. Her pay would add up to eight cents an hour. Not much, but she would at least get her flour and yeast.

When Sarah walked in the back door, she held the meat package out to Mama, who stood behind her ironing board.

"I have a present for you," she said.

"A present? My word! What could it be?" Her mother untied the white string and unfolded the pink butcher's paper.

"Sarah! Wherever did you get it?"

She explained about Mr. Neely's gift and his job offer.

Mama set the meat down on the stove edge and hugged her. "I never thought things would get so bad that you'd have to work for flour and yeast. But I'm proud of you, Sarah. And I'm sure Daddy will be, too."

Later Sarah and Mama found some wild onions growing among the roadside weeds. At supper that evening they ate the meat scraps that Mr. Neely had sent. Mama fried them with potatoes and the wild onion, making a delicious hash. Sarah had forgotten how good real beef smelled and tasted. Daddy told her how proud he was that she was finding a way to earn money. He hadn't found work that day, but he was keeping his promise. He never said a word about leaving them to go west.

48

7

c h a p t e r

ON HER WAY out of the store, Sarah stood in the door-way. "Thanks, Mr. Neely."

She carried two brown bags. One held a sack of flour and three cakes of yeast, her earnings for four days of after-school store cleaning. Tucked inside the other bag were Mr. Neely's gifts to her family. This afternoon there was a package of beef liver, a bunch of wilted carrots, and some sprouted potatoes. The grocer had also given her some extra paper sacks for her bread business.

He grinned at her. "Sure you can't come in to work again tomorrow?"

"I'm sure, Mr. Neely. I'm going to bake bread."

"Still set on sellin' that bread o' yours, huh?"

"You bet! Now that school's out, I'll have some extra time."

"Well, if you change your mind, you can always come back to work for me."

"Thanks." She was glad that Mr. Neely had liked her work. And he'd been good to her family. Each afternoon when she left his store, he had sent groceries home with her: things he was about to throw out—like blackened bananas and meat trimmings. Thanks to Mr. Neely, she and Mama and Daddy had eaten better these past few days than they had for a long time. And since Daddy hadn't found steady work, they'd needed that extra food.

As Sarah left with her bags of groceries, she saw Carla standing on the sidewalk in front of the store. She took a bag from Sarah.

"Here. I'll carry one of those. I can walk partway with you." Carla had been meeting Sarah after work. Twice she'd walked all the way home with her. The first time, Sarah had been afraid her friend would be shocked to see the house. But if she had been, she hadn't let on.

When they parted at the railroad tracks, Carla said, "Hope you sell all your bread tomorrow. Come to our house. I know my mother will buy some."

"I will. So long."

"See ya!"

Early the next afternoon Sarah stood at their kitchen table piling six loaves into two paper sacks. The bread had turned out well. She wished she could put each loaf into a separate bag, but since she couldn't count on getting any more from Mr. Neely she had decided against it.

When Mama had left to make laundry deliveries, she'd offered to give Sarah a ride in the truck, but the bread hadn't been quite done. Mama had gone out about half an hour earlier, but Daddy was there. After dinner at noon, he had gone to bed for a nap, saying he was tired. He'd looked for a job all morning, but found nothing. Sarah knew he sometimes slept because he was discouraged. To forget awhile. Some men without jobs went to afternoon movies for the same reason. On her way home from Mr. Neely's, Sarah would often see them filing out of the Aladdin after the matinee. But Daddy couldn't afford the quarter for a ticket.

Sarah felt rich. Mrs. Tilden had bought a loaf of her bread earlier that morning. Sarah had given her mother a nickel and put the remaining dime into her lucky box. Since she had earned all the flour and yeast for the new batch, she wouldn't have to pay Mama anything when it was sold. She'd have a whole dollar! And she'd used only half her supplies. She had enough flour and yeast left for another six loaves.

She'd never had a whole dollar before and didn't dare spend it all. To buy more supplies, she'd need to save thirty-nine cents. She hadn't quite decided what to do with the sixty-one cents' profit she would make that day. She might go to Mr. Neely's store and buy everything they'd need for a really good meal. It would be nice to have some bacon and eggs for a change. Or she could save the day's money, wait until she sold the next batch, and treat the family to a picture show and ice cream cones afterward. She'd let Mama and Daddy decide. She hoped they'd choose the picture show. It had been a long time since the family had gone out together for an evening of fun.

Before leaving, Sarah glanced through the open door of her parents' bedroom. Daddy was asleep. He'd taken off his shoes and thrown back the covers. His eyes were closed and his hands, folded across his chest, rose and fell with each slow breath. She wouldn't wake him to say good-bye.

51

Sarah decided to sell to the Petersons first, then go house to house in that same neighborhood. She'd take the short way. So what if she had to pass the Scully house? She'd gone by it a lot lately, and that gang hadn't even been there. Besides, she couldn't wait to sell the bread, and the two sacks made a clumsy load to carry very far. She'd take a chance.

From a half-block distance, she saw some kids sitting in the Scullys' front yard. Jake Scully was among them, seated on his rickety front porch. Had they seen her? They might have. She turned around and started to go the other way, but she heard footsteps pounding on the dirt road behind her. They were coming after her! She ran, the sacks rattling as she picked up speed. Without them she'd be able to go a lot faster, she thought. Panting, she tightened her grip on the bags and pushed on. The gang was catching up. How many were there? She hadn't had time to count them.

After a minute or so, Sarah felt someone tackle her from behind. She fell on the road face down. The sacks flew away from her as she landed on the heels of her hands. Then she saw the bags being snatched up. One loaf rolled in the dust and a kid dressed in patched pants scooped it up. There was a lot of whooping and shrieking.

"Look! Bread!" yelled one in a husky voice.

"Bread. Hey!" said another.

Sarah felt someone get off her back. She stood up and wiped the grit out of her eyes. Hate for this gang of toughs poured into every nerve. "Give me back my bread!" she yelled.

"Listen to Miss High and Mighty," said Jake in a sarcastic whine. He imitated her voice in a silly falsetto: "Give me back my bread." Then he took a big bite out of one of her loaves. His little sister and a dirty-faced boy each held a sack toward Sarah, but when she lunged at them, they snatched them back.

Anger tensed her muscles and she felt as if she could kill every last one of them. But at the same time, fear was turning her knees to jelly. Six of them surrounded her. She recognized one as the boy who lived two doors away from her. His sister, a girl about Sarah's age, was there too.

Sarah tried to remember Daddy's words. "Get so mad," he'd told her during the fighting lessons, "that you can't be scared." She was sure she could lick any one of them, but there were six. She was hurt and frightened and wanted to run, but knew they'd chase her. If she took on the smallest one, Jake's little sister, the big ones would rush to defend the girl. At least that's what Daddy had told her about facing a group. "Go after the biggest one," he'd said. "The others will probably just stand and watch."

She took a deep breath and decided to go after a brawny boy in a tight-fitting shirt. He was by far the biggest, and looked about fifteen. He took a bite out of one of her loaves. Then, with a silly grin, placed it on his head.

"How do you like my new hat?" he asked.

How dare he put her beautiful loaf on his dirty, greasy hair! In a rush of anger she made a tight fist and socked him on the chin. The loaf bounced off his head and rolled on the ground. The others did just what Daddy said they would: they stood there and waited for that big boy to finish her off. He staggered under Sarah's blow, then caught her by the wrists. She used the same trick on him she'd used on Jake that day at school, but with a different twist. While she thrust her wrists against his thumbs to free herself, she kicked him hard on his shin. He bent over and clutched his leg.

"Hey, take it easy," he yelled. But Sarah didn't. She made another fist and hit him on the nose. He lost his balance and fell to the ground. When a stream of blood ran down from his nostril and into his mouth, he licked his upper lip and spoke to the others as he got up. "C'mon. Let's get outa here!" Sarah noticed that the younger kids, in backing off, had left her sacks within easy reach. She grabbed them, whirled around, and ran. She could tell that they weren't following.

Sarah couldn't believe it. Daddy's battle plan, as he had called it, worked. It would be a while before any of them tried to tangle with her again. She'd run home right away, wake Daddy, and tell him all about it.

Sarah peeked inside the sacks. One had two loaves in it, the other only one. They looked untouched. She wouldn't be getting that dollar, but at least she'd been able to save three loaves. If she hadn't fought, every one of them would have been lost. Daddy would be proud of her.

As she headed home, Sarah felt the pain from her fall and cried some. Her knee was bloody and gray with road dust and stung terribly. So did one of her elbows. And she'd skinned the heels of her hands. She didn't know how many scrapes and bruises she had as she limped into their yard.

She noticed that the truck was still gone. Mama wasn't

home yet. She walked into the kitchen, calling to Daddy. But there was no answer, and the bedroom door was closed. That's strange, thought Sarah. The door had been open when she left. She remembered seeing him lying there with his arms crossed over his chest.

Sarah knocked and waited. No answer. "Daddy? Are you in there?" Silence. Slowly she opened the squeaky bedroom door. He was gone, and the bed was made up. That's odd. Daddy never made up the bed after a nap. He must have gone out to look for work again. But Mama had taken the truck. It wasn't like him to walk when he was job hunting.

Since nobody was home, Sarah decided to wash the dirt off her bruises and head out again. She'd take the long way to the Petersons' house and try to sell her three loaves. She wished Daddy was home to help her put on some iodine. She didn't have the nerve to put the stingy brown stuff on by herself.

Before leaving, Sarah walked into her parents' room again and stared at the made-up bed. She listened to the ticking of the kitchen clock, a lonely sound. Stroking the patchwork quilt where it had been drawn up over the pillows, Sarah heard a strange crackle. She threw back the covers and found a letter pinned to the pillow. It was two pages long, written in Daddy's hand, and dated yesterday. She unpinned it and started to read.

Dear Lucy and Sarah,
    As I write this, I'm sitting on a bench in the courthouse hall. You're not going to like what I have to

say, but I owe it to all of us to say it. The way I see it, I'm just kidding myself about finding a steady job in Waheegan. It's not going to happen, no matter how hard I try.

I know I promised not to talk about going out West again. Well, I didn't talk about it, but I have to write about it. If you think I'm breaking my word, I'm mighty sorry and hope to make it up to you one of these days.

To my way of thinking, it doesn't make a bit of sense to stay on here and do nothing while I eat up your share of the food. So I'm taking the first freight train west. All the way to California if I have to. By the time you read this, I should be on my way. There ought to be a decent job somewhere out there in this big country, and if there is, I intend to find it. When I get paid, I'll send you some of the money. Then as soon as I land a steady job, I'll mail you train tickets to wherever I am.

I have two reasons for sneaking off like this. First, if I stuck around to explain, I'd be breaking my promise. And second, I'd surely lose my nerve and might let myself be talked out of it. Believe me, I've done my share of moping over this, because I'll miss you both like crazy. But I have a feeling we'll all be back together again before the leaves turn brown this fall.

Lucy, I want you to take my gold watch and chain to Ed Schnabel down on 2nd Street. He'll most likely loan you ten dollars on it. You'll be needing that money for the rent and the electric bill. Don't worry about getting my watch back. I don't expect it.

Now you two keep on doing your best to stay alive, and don't worry about me. I'll be all right. And Sarah, now that school's out for the summer, you try and help your mother all you can.

I love you both,
Frank, Daddy.

Tears streamed down Sarah's face. How could Daddy do this to them? It wasn't fair! She wiped her eyes with the backs of her hands and read parts of the letter over again.

But why waste her time standing there, staring at the pages? He couldn't have been gone more than fifteen or twenty minutes. She threw her father's letter down on the bed and ran out the back door. Since he hadn't expected anyone to find his note so soon, there was a good chance he might still be at the train station. She'd hold on to his legs if she had to. Anything to keep him from leaving them. As she ran, a train whistle blew in the distance. Panic seized her. No! she thought. Please wait until I get there. Just five more minutes!

8

c h a p t e r

SARAH LOOKED DOWN the length of the tracks. No train in sight. The one that had whistled was gone, and Daddy was not among the people who stood near the rails.

Inside the station building she glanced around the room. He wasn't in there either. Several passengers waited on long benches, some with suitcases at their feet. Sarah studied the timetable on the wall. A west-bound freight train was due at 12:55 P.M. The wall clock above the ticket cage said 1:05. Did she dare hope that the train was late? But she'd heard its whistle. She knew that she had just missed it. Holding back her tears, she checked with the ticket man.

"Yep," he said. "Just went through about five minutes ago. Didn't stop. Just slowed down."

"Did you see a tall man in overalls get on?"

"Nope. If anybody tries to get on a boxcar around here, we order 'em off."

"Are there any more freight trains coming through?" Her voice quavered. Daddy might be waiting somewhere for a later one.

"Not here. Not till Monday."

58

Through a blur of tears, the ticket man's face melted into the window cage bars.

"You all right, young lady?" he asked.

Sarah nodded and turned away. A man who had been standing behind her moved up to the ticket counter. "What's wrong with the kid?" he whispered.

"Oh, some poor devil took off and left his family. We see a lot o' that now."

"Tough times."

"You're not kiddin'."

How dare those men talk about Daddy like that, as if he'd run away from them forever! And calling him a "poor devil." She ought to say something to them, but there wasn't time. Suppose Daddy hadn't sneaked onto the 12:55 after all? Maybe he'd decided to hitchhike. He might be standing on the road at the edge of town that very minute, trying to thumb a ride. If he was headed west, he'd be where Highway 50 joins Broad Street.

Sarah rushed out the station door and ran down Main Street to where it crossed Broad. She had to stop him. She turned west and ran the seven blocks to the edge of town, where the houses ended and the farms began.

Panting, she stared at the empty gravel road that stretched ahead and parted the grain fields. Nobody was there. The empty landscape yawned into the distance. Daddy was gone and there was nothing she could do about it.

As she walked toward home, she wondered if Mama knew yet, and what she would do. Suddenly her knee hurt again, and so did all her other scrapes and bruises. She felt tired and lonely, and wanted Mama. When she reached Main Street she ran the rest of the way.

Her mother sat at the kitchen table holding the letter. Her eyes, red-rimmed, stared wide from her pale face. "Here," she said when she saw Sarah, "this is to both of us."

"I've read it."

Mama and Sarah hugged each other. Sobbing, they said nothing for a long time. Then Sarah told Mama how she had searched the station and gone to look for Daddy on the road west of town.

"What are we going to do?" asked Sarah.

Mama spoke in a shaky voice. "First of all, I'll take a loan out on Daddy's watch and pay the rent and the electric bill. And if there's enough, maybe pay some to Mr. Neely at the grocery store. We'll just have to hang on the best we can." Mama glanced across the room to where Sarah's bread sacks lay on the cot. "I see you brought back some of your loaves." Sarah then explained what had happened with the neighborhood gang.

While her mother painted her scraped knee with iodine, Sarah held her breath and gritted her teeth.

"Mercy!" Mama shook her head. "And those hands! Here. Let's wash them again."

"Hurry, Mama," said Sarah. "I still want to go out and sell those three loaves."

"All right, but be careful. And please be back here before sundown."

"I will."

"While you're gone," said Mama, "I'll take Daddy's watch down to Mr. Schnabel."

Then they'd have ten dollars, Sarah thought. She could hardly imagine that much money.

Later that afternoon Sarah had sold her last loaf and walked toward home. She tried to keep her mind off Daddy by thinking about how quickly her bread had sold. She gripped the handkerchief into which she had tied five pennies, two nickels, and three dimes. Forty-five cents! Adding the ten cents she had at home in her lucky box, she now had fifty-five cents. If she saved thirty-nine cents for flour and yeast, she would have sixteen cents left. And when she sold the next six loaves made from the supplies she had on hand, she would have a whole dollar and six cents' profit. Sarah sighed. If those three loaves hadn't been stolen from her, she could have cleared a dollar and fifty-one cents.

When she passed the grocery store she thought about taking home a treat, but wasn't really hungry. The shock of Daddy's disappearance had taken away her appetite. She'd rather wait until she sold the next batch and take her mother to a picture show. She and Mama could both use a little cheering up.

Sarah's thoughts kept wandering back to Daddy. Suppose he had changed his mind after all and come back?

She found herself looking for him among the people on Main Street. She peered into all the store windows. No Daddy. But this was foolish, she told herself. He was gone, and she knew it. Yet the man at the station hadn't seen anyone get on that train. She allowed herself to imagine that when she got home her father would be sitting at the kitchen table reading the paper. With this picture in mind, she ran the rest of the way.

A quick glance into the dim kitchen told Sarah that Daddy wasn't there. She squinted into the twilight, confused to see Mama pouring oil into one of the kerosene lamps they had saved from the farm.

"Mama! What are you doing that for?" Sarah pulled the light chain, but the ceiling bulb didn't glow. She pulled it again. No light. "What's wrong? Did the bulb burn out?"

"The power company has cut us off." Mama lifted the lamp chimney, picked up a pair of scissors, and trimmed the wick.

"What do you mean?" asked Sarah.

"No more electricity until we pay our bill. We were warned last week."

Sarah stared at Mama across the table. "But you said you were going to pay our bills this afternoon. Didn't Mr. Schnabel give you the ten dollars for Daddy's watch?"

"Mr. Schnabel is a cheat and a scoundrel." Mama struck a match, lit the wick, and replaced the chimney. The lamp lit Mama's face from below, casting deep shadows under her eyes. "He offered me only three dollars. I refused."

"Three dollars? For Daddy's gold watch?"

"I couldn't believe it either. And he wouldn't listen to reason. So I walked out."

"Maybe somebody else will pay you more."

"I don't know. I'd have to see a jeweler, but there aren't any in Waheegan."

Sarah's mind raced. Mama wouldn't be able to run her washing machine without electricity, and washing so many clothes by hand would take too much time. She could still press clothes, because she heated the irons on the cookstove, but she'd probably make less money.

"How much is the electric bill?" Sarah asked.

Mama placed the lamp in the center of the table. "Three dollars."

"But Mama, if you took the three dollars from Mr. Schnabel, you could pay the electric bill and go on with the laundry and buy back the watch."

"It's not that simple, Sarah. Besides, I refuse to deal with that man."

Sarah was suddenly furious. At Mama for refusing perfectly good money, and at Daddy for leaving them. And at Mr. Schnabel and his cheap three-dollar offer. She ran out the back door, slamming it after her. She locked herself in the outhouse, sobbing and shaking as she leaned against the splintery wall.

After a time she heard Mama's voice just outside the door. "Are you all right, Sarah?"

"I guess so."

"Then come inside. We have some talking to do."

Whatever Mama had in mind to talk about wouldn't be

fun. Not after what had happened that day. She blew her nose and trudged into the house.

Mama was counting the coins in her cracked sugar bowl. Sarah looked on as her mother sorted the quarters, nickels, dimes, and pennies. She knew it was money they were going to discuss and she dreaded it. She wished she could just forget. She wanted to be like Carla. Carla never thought about money.

"We have three dollars and eighty-four cents," said Mama.

"Good," said Sarah. "Then you have enough to pay the electric bill and some to spare."

"No, Sarah. I have to save this for the rent." Mama put the coins back in with a clinking sound while Sarah stared at the sugar bowl. The crack lines made tiny x's through the bouquet of flowers on its side.

"We have no choice," said Mama. "We have to pay the rent first. Electricity is out of the question."

Sarah felt dizzy. Why did her mother have to talk to her about these things? She was just a kid. Sarah said nothing, hoping Mama would change the subject.

But her mother went on to explain. "The rent was due almost two weeks ago, and we couldn't pay the landlord when he came. He'll probably be back on Monday."

They really needed that ten dollars Daddy tried to leave them, Sarah thought. Why hadn't he taken out a loan on the watch himself and left them the money? Maybe he wouldn't have gone away if he'd known it would bring only three dollars.

"What'll happen if we don't pay it?"

"The landlord could force us to leave."

Sarah swallowed hard. "Where would we go?"

"The county sends people like us to the poorhouse, Sarah."

"What's a poorhouse?" Sarah wondered if anything could be worse than the house they were living in.

"A big building near the edge of town," said Mama, "where people go who can't make a living. Where you work for your room and board and do farm chores to raise food. It's a terrible place."

"Like a jail?"

"Something like a jail. I hear they are dirty, crowded places, filled with mean, foul-mouthed people." Mama's voice cracked.

It would be like moving into the same house with that nasty neighborhood gang, thought Sarah. Only worse. Whatever happened, they had to stay out of the poorhouse.

She couldn't imagine Carla in a place like that. Why did she keep thinking about Carla? Her friend had nothing to do with all this. Maybe that was why she kept thinking about her. She wanted to be like her. But she *was* like her in so many ways. It wasn't fair. Why couldn't she be rich like Carla? None of it made sense.

"Have you paid Mr. Neely the five dollars we owe?" she asked.

"No," said Mama. "But he lets us buy things as long as we pay cash."

The oil lamp flickered. Sarah watched shadows dip and dance on the walls. She had known all along that they were terribly poor, but she now realized for the first time just

65

how desperate their situation was. Though Daddy had been out of work, she had always felt as if he stood between them and total disaster. But he was gone. It was as if she and Mama were being carried down a swollen river alone in a leaky boat.

Mama got up from the table, put the sugar bowl back up on the windowsill, and filled a cooking pot with water.

"What are we having for supper?" asked Sarah.

"Rice."

"I sold four loaves of bread today, Mama. I have to save thirty-nine cents for more flour and yeast, but I have sixteen cents to spare. We could buy a can of salmon and a few carrots or a cabbage."

"Thanks, dear, but Mr. Neely has probably closed his store by this time."

The only bright spot in this terrible day, Sarah thought, had been the ease with which she sold her bread. At every door she visited, she'd sold a loaf. She was sure that if she'd had six loaves they would have gone just as fast. Or twelve. Or maybe even twenty-four.

Sarah tore a sheet from her school tablet, got a pencil, and multiplied fifteen cents by twenty-four. Three dollars and sixty cents. If she sold twenty-four loaves every day six days a week, that would be twenty-one dollars and sixty cents minus the cost of flour and yeast. She could make sixteen dollars and ninety-two cents' clear profit! Enough to pay off their debts and buy whatever they needed, even electricity. Excited, she showed the figures to her mother.

Mama paused in her cooking and listened, cocking her

head as Sarah went through the math. Mama made some notes on another sheet of tablet paper and studied them.

"But Sarah, we'd have to make two batches of twelve loaves each. The day wouldn't be long enough to make four batches of six. You've never tried to make that much at once."

Sarah opened the oven door and placed all their bread pans—six of them—on the top shelf. Then she placed them on the bottom one. It was a deep oven, and held them all. "See? There's room for twelve loaves at a time. If you helped me, I bet we could do it in two batches."

Mama smiled a bit. "You have a good idea there, Sarah. But we have only six pans."

"Maybe we could borrow some."

"Since I've started with the laundry business, I should probably go on with it. After all, I have my customers."

"But Mama, you can't use your washing machine now."

"I could take in ironing. And maybe do some mending. Since you've done the baking for so long, I don't know if I'd be any good at it."

"I could teach you, Mama. It's not that hard."

"That's true, but—"

"How much money does the laundry make?"

"With the machine, I cleared about four dollars a week after expenses. Sometimes less."

"Mama, baking would be a lot better."

Mama studied Sarah's face. "I'd like to believe that, honey. It's possible, you know, that you may have had beginner's luck this afternoon. Suppose we couldn't sell all that bread after we bake it?"

"I'll bet we can."

Mama stared into the distance, and her lips began to tremble. She sank into a chair, put her head on the table, and sobbed. Watching her mother's grief, Sarah was hit again by the events of the afternoon, and she couldn't help but cry too.

Soon Mama composed herself and raised her head. "I'm sorry," she said, "but it's been such a hard day."

Sarah wiped away her own tears, then got up and put her hands on Mama's shoulders. "I have enough flour and yeast left for six more loaves. I'm going to get up early in the morning and start a batch. We can take it to church with us in the truck, and sell it afterward."

"To church?" Her mother looked surprised.

"Mama, I won't sell it at the church if you don't want me to. We can do it later. House to house, maybe. Please?"

Her mother blew her nose and drew in a long, shaky breath. Then she patted Sarah's hand. "You're right. We'll have to raise some money tomorrow, Sunday or no Sunday, and it's the best idea we've come up with. We'll have to try it. I'll get up and help you. When should we start?"

"Five o'clock."

"I'll set the alarm."

Lying awake, Sarah waited until Mama stopped sniffling in the next room. Then she slipped out of bed and pulled her lucky box out from under her cot. She reached for a dime, a nickel, and a penny, the money she had been saving for tomorrow's picture show. For now, she might as well forget about movies and ice cream. The poorhouse hung over her thoughts like a black cloud.

She walked over to the windowsill and dropped the coins into Mama's sugar bowl. They now needed one more dollar to pay the rent. If all went well, and she sold six loaves after church, they would have ninety cents more the next day. They had until Monday to worry about that last dime. If they had any food at all on their shelves, they could live on it until then.

Sarah had made up her mind about one thing. No matter what, she didn't dare dip into the thirty-nine cents she was saving for flour and yeast. She'd go hungry first. It was what Daddy always called seed money. On the farm, you had to save enough to plant the next year's crop. Without seed money, all hope could slip away.

9

c h a p t e r

AFTER SERVICES THE next morning, several people came up to Mama and Sarah, who stood near the front steps of the church. Some asked where Daddy was. Mama told them he was looking for work and said no more.

As planned, Sarah and Mama had gotten up at five o'clock to bake. Sarah had been happy to have Mama's help, since her hands were still sore from yesterday's fall. She had shown her mother exactly how to mix and knead the dough, and Mama had done well. On the front seat of their truck, six golden loaves, piled into two grocery bags, waited to be sold. They planned to sell them house to house after church.

But a surprising thing happened. Mrs. Stoddard, one of the women to whom Sarah had sold bread the day before, came rushing up to her. She was with another woman whom she introduced as Mrs. McGinnis.

"You'll have to meet this young lady," said Mrs. Stoddard to her friend. "She bakes the most delicious home-made bread. I bought some yesterday. And if you put in an order, she might come by your house." She turned to Sarah. "You wouldn't happen to have any more, would you? I have company coming for Sunday dinner and could use another loaf."

This was a real break, thought Sarah. She looked up at Mama, who smiled and nodded. "If you'll come with me," said Sarah, "I'll sell you some." The four of them went to the truck, which was parked in front of the church.

While Sarah exchanged two loaves for thirty cents, another friend of Mrs. Stoddard's stopped by and bought a loaf, too. As the church emptied, a small group gathered around the truck. In a few minutes the bread was gone, and Sarah handed her mother ninety cents.

Mama stared at the money. "It's unbelievable. The bread went so fast!"

Sarah grinned. "Mama, we didn't even have to knock on doors!"

"I think you have something here, Sarah." Mama cranked the truck, and they climbed in.

"Do you want to go home and make another batch?" Sarah asked.

Mama bit her lip. "I'm usually against working on Sunday, you know. But since we still owe a dime on the rent, we really have no choice."

"Oh, oh!" Sarah said. "I just remembered. We're out of flour and yeast."

"And the grocery store is closed on Sunday," said Mama.

"I have the money for it, though," said Sarah. "I'll bet Mr. Neely would open the store if I asked him to. I know where he lives."

"Do you have your money with you?"

"No. It's at home in my lucky box."

"Let's go get it."

As Sarah and her mother drove into their yard, they saw four or five members of the neighborhood gang clustered around the kitchen door. The screen was open, resting against the intruders' backs.

Sarah's muscles tightened and her throat went dry. "What are they doing here?"

"I don't know," said Mama, "but I don't like it." Her face had gone white. Four of the gang members, including the one whose nose Sarah had bloodied the day before, whirled around when they heard the truck coming. Then they dashed around the corner of the house, leaving behind Jake Scully, whose shoulder was leaning against the wooden door. A second later he spun around, jumped off the steps, and followed the others.

Were they going in or out? Sarah wondered. It looked as if they had been on their way in, but she couldn't be sure. If they had been in the house, what about the money? Had they stolen it?

As she and Mama ran up to the house, Sarah saw that the back door was standing ajar, and the screen had a hole in it where something had been pushed through to pry up the hook.

"Mama, they broke the inside lock," Sarah cried. "Look!" She pointed to the frail bar fastener, which hung at an angle from the edge of the wooden door. They had

72

pushed it out of the frame, screws and all, leaving a splintery hole. Sarah dashed through the kitchen to the front room and peered out the window. She saw several figures running toward the road, Jake Scully among them. "Mama, there they go!"

Her mother hurried to the kitchen windowsill. "The rent money!" She picked up the sugar bowl and heaved an enormous sigh. "Looks as if the money's still here." Her voice trembled. She dumped the coins out on the kitchen table and counted them. "Four dollars. And with the money we just made, that makes four dollars and ninety cents. Thank God! We must have caught them just before they got in."

Sarah looked under her cot and pulled out her lucky box. She was relieved to see that the thirty-nine cents still sat atop her blue ribbon. "Mama, I think I'll take my lucky box over to Carla's. It'll be safer at her house."

"Good idea," said Mama. "And I'm carrying my money with me. From now on, any extra earnings will go into the bank." She poured the money from the sugar bowl into a coin purse and put it in her handbag. Then she went into the bedroom. "I'm taking Daddy's watch with me, too. After we buy our flour, I'll drop by the sheriff's office and tell him what happened." Before they left, they piled chairs against the back door.

Instead of unlocking the store for them, Mr. Neely sold them an unopened ten-pound sack of flour and three pack-

73

ets of yeast his wife happened to have in the house. He seemed pleased that Sarah had sold her bread and was getting ready to bake more.

After leaving Mr. Neely's house, they dropped by the Petersons', where Sarah left her lucky box with Carla for safekeeping. And since Mrs. Peterson no longer baked bread, she gladly loaned Sarah six bread pans. They had been gathering dust on her kitchen shelf, she said. She told Sarah to keep them as long as she needed them.

Next Sarah and Mama went to see the sheriff. He didn't seem too interested in what the neighborhood kids had done, especially since they hadn't stolen anything. He suggested that Mama buy a good lock for the back door. Neither she nor Sarah said a word about not being able to afford one. It was too embarrassing.

When they got home, they found the kitchen door as they had left it. The gang hadn't been back. Since she and Mama had caught them in the act, thought Sarah, they might not try anything like that again. Still, Sarah felt uneasy about living in such a neighborhood with no lock on the back door.

But she had more exciting things to think about. She and Mama were going to make and sell twelve loaves of bread that afternoon. When the landlord came the next day, they'd be ready for him.

10

chapter

LATER THAT SUNDAY afternoon, Sarah and Mama took their bread out of the cookstove. They had squeezed twelve pans into the oven all at once, six on each shelf. By shifting the loaves around when they were half done, they had managed to bake the whole batch perfectly. Mama had been afraid they might not be able to sell all the bread that afternoon, and suggested they start by baking only six loaves, but Sarah convinced her that they should try twelve.

They had taken the chairs away from the back door to open it. In spite of the fresh air, the kitchen was so hot that beads of sweat rolled down Sarah's neck and the insides of her arms, and she felt exhausted. Mama wore a kerchief tied around her forehead to keep the perspiration from rolling onto the bread. But the loaves looked wonderful. Sarah breathed in their yeasty scent.

In an hour or so they would have the whole five dollars for the house rent and more to spare! She couldn't wait. The poorhouse haunted her thoughts.

At her back, there was a knock at the door. Startled, Sarah jumped. Suppose it was the landlord? But they weren't expecting him until Monday. Surely he wouldn't come on a Sunday. She spun around and saw a heavyset man standing outside the screen. Since Mama was busy at the oven, Sarah stepped toward him.

"Is your mother or father in?" asked the man in a gravelly voice. Though he was clean shaven, his heavy beard lay just under his skin, darkening his lower face. Curly black hair covered his arms and sprouted from the open collar of his short-sleeve shirt.

Please, God, Sarah silently prayed, Don't let this be the landlord. "Mama! Somebody's at the door." She went back to her pans of bread.

"Oh!" Mama glanced at the man, then at Sarah, a look of alarm spreading across her face. "Come in, Mr. Cross. I'll get the rent money." Mama hurried into the bedroom. So it was the landlord, thought Sarah. And his name was Mr. Cross! Sarah's stomach quivered. She wondered whether he would throw them out if he didn't get the whole five dollars right then.

Mama came back with her handbag. "I have the money right here. All except one dime. And I'll have that later this afternoon." Sarah held her breath and crossed her fingers for luck.

Their landlord shook his head and heaved a big sigh. "Ma'am, I just can't believe that after all this time, you're still not able to scrape up the whole five dollars."

"But Mr. Cross," said Mama, "I promise I'll bring you that last dime this afternoon."

"Oh, I believe you," he said. "It's just that I'm worried about next month's rent and the month after that. You folks have been awful slow paying. When I came last week you didn't have it, and it was a week late then. And you didn't have it the week before that, on the first, when it came due. And now it's two weeks late, and you're still havin' trouble scrapin' it together. If you can't save five dollars in six weeks, how can I expect you to have it ready in two weeks when it comes due again on the first?"

Mama's face had gone pale. "We'll try, Mr. Cross."

"I 'spect you're havin' your troubles like a lot o' folks around here," said Mr. Cross. "The Depression has been hard on everybody, but I got bills to pay too. And I can't do it on late rent and short funds. Where's your mister? I wanta talk to him."

"He's out of town right now."

"Outa town, huh? Still lookin' for work?"

"Yes."

"Look," he said, "with your husband skippin' town you're what I consider a pretty bad risk."

Sarah couldn't stand the way Mr. Cross spoke about Daddy "skipping town" as if he were some kind of criminal.

"Tell you what," said Mr. Cross. "I had a feeling things were gettin' pretty shaky for you folks. I said to myself as I was drivin' up here, if they don't have all the money together this afternoon, I'm gonna call it quits, 'cause I could put a good payin' renter in this place tomorrow. I have a helper in my truck out there. He'll move your stuff for you and haul it to wherever you say. If you ask me, that's a pretty generous offer. You got relatives in town?"

Fear crept up Sarah's spine.

Mama drew herself up tall. "No, Mr. Cross, we have no relatives here. Give us a chance please. In one hour you will get the rest of your money."

Mr. Cross spoke softly. "I've been pretty patient up to now, Mrs. Puckett. And I sympathize. Believe me, I do. But there's a limit. When you start givin' in to an hour here and an hour there when the rent is already two weeks late, I'd say we're dealin' with a situation that's not apt to get any better. The county runs a place out on the edge o' town for people who can't pay rent."

He was talking about the poorhouse! To steady herself, Sarah grasped the edge of the table. She stared at the loaf she had just slipped out of the pan. If only it would magically turn into fifteen cents right this minute. Or even a dime. She had an idea.

"Mr. Cross," she said, "I was going to sell this loaf of bread for fifteen cents. If you took it now instead of a dime, you'd be a nickel ahead."

He studied her face. "You runnin' a bakery in here?"

Sarah didn't know how to answer his question. She looked at Mama, whose mouth stood partway open, as if all speech had been scared out of her. Sarah wondered if running a bakery might be another reason for Mr. Cross to throw them out.

After a long pause, Mama spoke. "We're just getting a start. We go house to house. We don't do any selling here. Just the baking."

Mr. Cross frowned, studied the floor, then looked Mama squarely in the face. "Think you can make a go of it?"

78

"I hope so," said Mama. "Sarah here is a champion baker. She won a blue ribbon at the county fair last year."

Mr. Cross turned to Sarah. "You a hard worker?"

"Yes, sir," Sarah said. Please, she thought, let him give us another chance!

"All right." He held out his hand. "This time I'll take the bread and your four dollars and ninety cents. But don't let it happen again." A flood of relief washed over Sarah as she handed him the loaf. He held the bread in one hairy hand while Mama counted out the money into the other.

He pocketed the coins. "I hope you understand, Mrs. Puckett. If you run short or you're late next month, you'll have to move. No two ways about it. I'll be here June first, two weeks from now, and I expect to collect the whole five dollars." He walked toward the door, then turned around. "By the way, it smells mighty good in here. I wish you luck with your new business."

From the open door Sarah and Mama watched Mr. Cross and his helper drive away. In spite of the heat, Sarah trembled as if she were having a chill. Then she felt Mama's arms wrap around her and hold her close.

As their truck chugged down an avenue of large homes, two grocery bags of bread sat between Sarah and Mama on the front seat, and Sarah held two sacks in her lap.

"Try to find out who lives next door to the people you're selling to," Mama said. "Folks like to be called by their names, so introduce yourself. Say, 'Mrs. Smith or Mrs.

79

Jones, I'm Sarah Puckett, and I have some homemade bread to sell.' "

It seemed to Sarah that Mama was making a big fuss over little things. But she soon learned that it wasn't just good manners her mother was teaching.

"You should know the names of your customers," Mama said, "and remember them. It's good business."

Each time Sarah sold a loaf, Mama, waiting in the truck, wrote the name and address of the customer in a little notebook. In a short time the eleven loaves were sold, and Mama and Sarah had a dollar and sixty-five cents.

If it had been a weekday, they would have stopped off at Neely's grocery for food. They were hungry and had nothing left to eat in the house except a little oatmeal. Instead they went to the drugstore, the only place open on a Sunday evening, and spent a quarter on a pint of ice cream. It was the only food they could buy in Waheegan. Sarah was glad. If Neely's had been open, they wouldn't be having such a treat that night.

"We'll have to go home and celebrate our success," Mama said.

Sarah smiled. She wondered what Daddy would have thought about the day's happenings. As they drove down Main Street, she looked for him. She knew it was silly, but she couldn't help it.

"I was thinking," said Mama, "at the rate we're going, we should have next month's rent saved by week's end."

"That's wonderful, Mama."

"And if we bake at least two batches a day and sell all twenty-four loaves, we should bring in enough money to

80

pay our bills and get along. I wasn't able to do that with the laundry. When you sell bread, you don't have to wait so long to get paid. And the kitchen is no hotter, really. I had to build fires to heat the irons anyway. After today, I wouldn't even consider going back to ironing."

"Good." Sarah smiled. She was pleased that the figures she had jotted down on paper the night before hadn't lied to them.

"We'll both have to work very hard. I don't think one person could possibly do it. Shall we try?"

"Sure, Mama. And don't forget to save enough for flour and yeast."

Mama patted her knee. "You're right. That's very important."

"Go faster, Mama, so we can eat our ice cream before it melts."

Mama smiled and speeded up a bit. "That's a good idea."

Sarah ran a spoon around her nearly empty dish and licked off the last sweet drops of ice cream. They had checked the house when they came in. Nothing had been disturbed.

"Do you think those kids will break into our house again, Mama?"

"I don't know, Sarah. I doubt it, but we'll have to stay alert and do what we can to discourage them."

Sarah shuddered. "I feel creepy about it."

"Yes, I know," said Mama. "Let's try not to dwell on it."

But Sarah was afraid, and the gloomy shadows cast by

81

the kerosene lamp saddened her. She thought about Daddy and wondered where he was. She missed him terribly. Whenever she closed her eyes she saw him. Sometimes he sat across the table from her. Other times he was walking across the yard. Or they were sitting together on the riverbank, fishing. It was late evening, the time he was usually home with them. She looked up, half expecting to hear him open the screen door. She remembered how the floor creaked under his footsteps. "Mama, where do you think Daddy is now?"

"I don't know, Sarah. We'll just have to be patient."

Before they went to bed Mama closed the back door and piled chairs against it. She put her coin purse, filled with the day's earnings, under her pillow.

Sarah slept in snatches, keeping one ear cocked for intruders. In one of her dreams a freight train stopped at the Waheegan station. Sarah went on board and pulled Daddy out of a boxcar. In another dream she and her father went hunting together. Sarah had the gun. Daddy ran away from her just as she shot a rabbit.

Mama and Sarah got up at dawn the next morning. Sarah couldn't wait for Neely's store to open. They had enough money to buy some food as well as more flour and yeast.

For breakfast, Mama cooked the last of the oatmeal. As they ate, Sarah told her mother that she had dreamed about Daddy.

"I dreamed about him too," said Mama. "But we'll be

hearing from him soon." She quickly changed the subject. "You and I have a lot to do, young lady. This is the day we bake twenty-four loaves of bread and try to sell them. Think we can do it?"

Through her tears, Sarah grinned and nodded.

11

chapter

THE POSTMAN WALKED slowly toward the house, his brown leather bag slung over his shoulder. In his hand, he held several envelopes. Sarah ran down the road to meet him.

Please, oh, please, Sarah thought, let one of those letters be from Daddy telling us he's found a good job! During the past six weeks he had written them five postcards. Each had said about the same thing: "I'm thinking of you," "No steady work yet," or "Dug ditches today. Nothing steady." Another time: "Helped a farmer with wheat harvest. Only three days' work." Four of the cards were postmarked from small towns in Colorado and Utah. The last one was from Needles, California. California! The very name of that state spelled magic and adventure in Sarah's mind. He'd surely have better luck there. But they'd heard nothing since.

"No letter today," said the mail carrier.

"Not even a card? Are you sure?" asked Sarah.

He shuffled through the envelopes in his hand. "Nope, 'fraid not."

How odd, thought Sarah. It had been ten days since they'd heard from him. Until then he had written them every week. Slowly she turned and walked toward the house.

In the worst way, she wanted Daddy to send for them. She missed him, of course. But there was another reason. She was tired of work. She was exhausted, and dreamed of a nice trip west. What fun it would be to ride through the mountains on a train. She'd never been on a train and had never seen mountains. If they went to California, there'd be the Pacific Ocean. She'd never seen an ocean, either.

At home there was too much baking. It was hard, hot work, and the hours were long. Even though Mama saw to it that she had a little time off every day, Sarah couldn't help noticing the difference between her life and Carla's. Sarah's friend hardly worked at all. She cleaned her room now and then, and ran a dustcloth over the living room furniture on Saturdays. Otherwise she played and read and practiced the piano. Afternoons when they were together, she and Carla often pretended to be real sisters. Sometimes Sarah wished they were.

During the past six weeks, Mama and Sarah had been making twenty-four loaves of bread a day. Except on Sunday, of course. They got up at the crack of dawn to mix, knead, and bake. Later in the morning they did the same thing all over again. Her mother then drove her in the truck while Sarah knocked on doors. Almost no one turned her down. If there was any time left before supper, she visited Carla. At sundown Sarah and her mother fell into bed, exhausted.

The heat from the kitchen met Sarah with a blast as she

85

opened the screen door. Mama, flushed and perspiring, with a kerchief tied around her forehead, was taking the first batch out of the oven. "Did we get a card from Daddy?" she asked.

"No, Mama."

Her mother wiped her face with her forearm. "That's strange," she said. "He usually writes every week." Then she bent over the oven. "Here, Sarah, take these out of the pans to cool."

"In a minute." Work, work, work, thought Sarah. But she said nothing. She filled a bucket from the sink and carried it outdoors to the side of the house. She lifted the pail high, closed her eyes, and poured it over her head. Her clothes and hair dripping wet, she went back into the kitchen. To stay cool she and Mama poured water over themselves every hour or so. Wetting their clothes and hair allowed them to work in that furnace of a kitchen without getting sick.

They had been lucky, Sarah thought. The last two times Mr. Cross had come to the door they were ready for him with the full five dollars, and they now had enough money to buy the food they needed. Mama had insisted that they pay Mr. Neely what they owed him before having the electricity hooked up, and last week they had lights again. But when Sarah had worked out their business on paper that night after Daddy left, she had no idea what twenty-four loaves a day would mean in sore muscles, heat, and bone-melting tiredness.

Sarah slipped the twelve new loaves out of their pans onto cooling racks. Though she still liked the smell of fresh-baked bread, she'd be just as happy if she never had to make another loaf. But Mama never complained, so Sarah didn't either.

Her mother had quite a head for business. Early that morning she had driven the truck down to a mill at the edge of town where she bought a hundred-pound sack of flour. In the long run, she told Sarah, it was cheaper than buying it in small packages from Mr. Neely's store. The people at the mill told her how to order yeast and wrapping paper at wholesale prices. Mama recorded all their baking expenses and earnings in an account book, and kept a long list of their customers' names and addresses. Their bank account was growing, too.

They were no longer as frightened as they had been. A month ago, just after they had paid the rent, Mr. Cross put a lock on their back door. The neighborhood gang never broke into their house again. Nor had they bothered Sarah when she walked past their hangout in front of the Scully place. Daddy had been right. Fighting them was the thing to do.

Sarah sighed as she helped Mama fill the pans for the next batch. Another day, another dollar, she thought. If they met Daddy in California, they might live in a house on the seashore where they could swim and enjoy the cool ocean breezes. She tried to imagine the sound of the waves breaking against the shore.

That evening at supper Mama talked to Sarah about the business. She seldom talked about anything else. She never said much about Daddy unless Sarah brought up the subject.

"I've been thinking," Mama said, "about how much time I waste driving you around to the different neighborhoods. We could make more money if our customers came to us."

"People wouldn't want to come here, Mama. Besides, Mr. Cross might not like it."

"No, you're right. But if I had more time, I could experiment with cinnamon rolls. And if we had a place to sell from, think of all the gasoline we could save."

"Cinnamon rolls?" Sarah couldn't believe her ears.

"Yes," said Mama. "We could use your basic bread recipe, add a few ingredients, and charge twenty-five cents for a half dozen."

That sounds great, Mama." Sarah loved cinnamon rolls, and making something different would be a change from the same dull routine.

"We'd need a place," said Mama. "But where?"

"There's an empty store building downtown. Mr. Willard owns it."

Mama sighed. "He'd charge rent. Plenty, too, since it's on Main Street."

"You could ask him about it."

"No, Sarah, it's out of the question. I can't take on any more expenses. We're doing all right, but we need every penny."

Sarah had always dreamed about that building. She'd say nothing about it now, but it wouldn't hurt to go see Mr. Willard, at least to ask the price. It might not be any more than they were spending for gas. If Mama wouldn't do it, she would. It would be fun to sell bread and cinnamon rolls on Main Street. Besides, going door to door was tiresome.

But another thought was troubling her. "Mama, I wonder why Daddy hasn't written us. It's been ten days."

"I know. I hope he's all right." Mama stared at the loaf of bread on the table. The tiny lines around her mouth deepened. Her mother was worried, Sarah could tell.

12

chapter

THE NEXT MORNING, while the first batch of bread was rising at home, Sarah stood in front of Mr. Willard's empty building on Main Street. The faded sign, FOR RENT OR SALE, was still tucked into one of the windows. Sarah peered through the glass. Dust and cobwebs had gathered on the display shelves behind the big panes. Beyond them a huge space yawned, mostly shadowed and hidden. Dark wood shelves, littered with trash, lined both walls. Broken furniture, torn boxes, and wads of paper nearly covered the wood floor. Whoever had moved out had made an awful mess.

Sarah did some hard thinking. The store was a lot larger than anything they needed, but if it were cleaned up, she and Mama could display their bread (and cinnamon rolls) in those windows. She could sit by them instead of knocking on doors. Since the store was downtown, where lots of people walked by every day, their bread should sell quickly. They couldn't afford rent of course, so she had come up with a scheme, one that had worked before. But she hadn't told Mama about it.

Her throat went dry when she thought about going to see Mr. Willard. What if he laughed at her because she was a kid? So what? she thought. People had laughed at her before. If Mr. Willard turned her down, she and Mama wouldn't be any worse off. Sarah took a deep breath. It was worth a try.

At the hardware store Sarah's heart pounded in her ears. Mr. Willard's wife, who was one of Sarah's customers, stood at the counter.

"Why, Sarah, what can I do for you?" she asked.

"I'd like to talk to Mr. Willard." Her voice shook a little.

"Well, if it's hardware you want," said Mrs. Willard, "I know as much as he does. We've both been in this business twenty years. By the way," she said, "we liked that bread you sent over the other evening. When are you comin' by again?"

"That's why I want to talk to Mr. Willard," said Sarah.

"Well, young lady, I'm afraid you're barkin' up the wrong tree. My husband don't know beans about bread. If you ask me, I don't think he knows the difference between beans and bread. He just eats whatever I set out. Never says a word, just chomps it down. So if it's bread you have on your mind, you'd better talk to me."

"It isn't exactly about bread." Sarah was losing her nerve and was about to walk out the door when a plump, bald man came in from a back room.

"Henry," said Mrs. Willard, "Sarah Puckett's here. You know, the bread girl. Says she wants to talk to you about something."

"W-e-l-l!" Mr. Willard held out his hand. He looked

91

like a nice man who was used to smiling a lot. "So you're the young lady who bakes that fine bread we've had lately. Been wanting to meet you."

After what Mrs. Willard had just said, Sarah wasn't sure she could believe his kind words. But she grinned and took his hand. She liked his friendliness.

"You know that building you own across from Neely's?" After the words came out, she felt her face burn. What a silly question!

"I oughta know it," he said. "For months now I've been tryin' to rent it or sell it. No takers, though."

Sarah swallowed and spoke the words she'd practiced on the way over. "Mr. Willard," she said, "I could sweep it out for you. And wash the windows and dust and make it look nice."

"Well, I'll tell you, Sarah," said Mr. Willard, "you have a good idea there. But I just don't have the money to hire anybody to do that kind of work right now, and my wife and I don't have time to do it ourselves."

"You wouldn't have to pay me money, Mr. Willard."

"Well, if you don't want money, what do you want?" he asked.

Sarah cleared her throat and blurted it out. "I'd like to put our bread in your show windows for a couple of hours a day."

Mr. Willard looked at her and stroked his chin. "Hmmm. Are you pretty good at cleaning?"

Sarah smiled at him. "I cleaned Mr. Neely's store and he thought I was."

Mr. Willard turned to his wife. "Whatta ya think, Rose?

92

If the place starts lookin' better, somebody might want to rent it or buy it."

Mrs. Willard smiled at him. "Go ahead, Henry. What harm could it do?"

Mr. Willard spoke as if he were thinking out loud. "Of course, I'll have to leave that sign in the window."

Sarah held her breath.

Mr. Willard grinned. "You have a deal, young lady. You keep the place clean and lookin' nice, and you can sell your bread there free o' charge. That is until somebody buys it or rents it. When do you want to move in?"

Breathless, she replied, "As soon as I get it cleaned up, Mr. Willard. This afternoon!" Sarah managed to stand there quiet as a grown-up. But inside she was dancing and yelling and turning somersaults.

Later that morning Mrs. Willard unlocked the door for Sarah and her mother.

"Look, Mama. It'll be perfect!" Sarah cried. Her voice echoed in the emptiness, and the building smelled dank and musty.

"It's wonderful, Sarah," said Mama.

Mrs. Willard smiled. "I'll be going now. Sarah, will you be in here alone?" When Sarah nodded, Mrs. Willard tucked her key into her handbag. "Well, whenever you're ready to leave, let me know, and I'll come back and lock up." Sarah couldn't understand why Mrs. Willard didn't leave the key with her. It would save her a lot of trouble, but she probably didn't trust a kid that much.

From the truck Mama and Sarah carried in a broom, a mop, rags, buckets, and soap.

"I can't believe it!" Mama said, hugging Sarah. "You actually got this place for us, when I was too timid to try." Mama released her. "But suppose they rent or sell the store out from under us?"

"We wouldn't be any worse off. We can always go back to selling from the truck."

"I suppose you're right. It'll give me more time for baking, at least for a while. And it'll save gas." Mama stood inside the building and looked around. "It's enormous. And very dirty. Do you think you can clean it all by yourself? I'll have to go home and finish the bread."

"I'm going to call Carla. She'll help."

"How long do you think it will take you?"

"Three or four hours, probably."

"Hmmm," said Mama. "If I bring the bread down here at four, we should be able to sell it by six. I'm going to the drugstore now to call some of our customers so they'll know where to find us." Mott's Drug had a free phone. Sarah had often used it to call Carla. As Mama turned to go, Sarah suddenly realized she wouldn't be home when the postman came.

"Mama?" called Sarah. "I hope we get a card from Daddy today."

Mama's brows came together. "I hope so too."

Sarah stood on a ladder she'd found in the back of the building. With a broom she knocked cobwebs off the pounded tin ceiling. She and Carla had already swept the floors and carried out what seemed like tons of trash.

The place is huge, Sarah thought. Must be forty feet from front to back.

Carla was washing one of the large show windows. Her voice echoed through the store. "You know what you need in here?"

"No, what?" Sarah brushed damp hair from her forehead.

"An electric fan. It's hot."

"We'll have to wait a while, I guess." Sarah felt annoyed with Carla sometimes. Since she'd always had everything she wanted, it was hard for her to imagine doing without.

"Look, Sarah." Carla pointed to the curtain rods running across the windows. "You should have some bright-colored cloth to hang up there. It would make a big difference."

Sarah sighed. Didn't her friend realize that yard goods cost money?

"And you ought to have a sign," said Carla.

Sarah smiled. "A sign would be nice. Maybe I can make one sometime." Carla jumped off the display platform by the window and went to the door.

"Where are you going?" asked Sarah.

"Home. But I'll be back."

"Well, 'bye. And thanks for the help." It must be about one o'clock, Sarah thought. Carla might be hungry. Or need a rest. She wasn't used to hard work.

In half an hour Carla came back to the store carrying a big cardboard box. She set it down on the window display

95

platform. Sarah had been mopping what seemed like miles of rough wooden floor.

"Carla, what do you have in there?"

"Come here and I'll show you." Carla opened the box flaps. Sarah dropped the mop handle with a clack and ran over to where her friend stood. From the box Carla took out a piece of cardboard and some watercolors. "For a sign to put in the window," she said. Next she pulled out a small electric fan, placed it on the seat of a backless chair they'd saved from the rubbish pile, and plugged it into a wall outlet. "Mother said you can borrow it for the summer. It was in our basement. We don't use it much since we bought larger ones."

Sarah squealed and knelt in front of the fan, stretching out her arms to enjoy the breeze. Then Carla went back to the box and pulled out pieces of red-checked cloth.

"My mother made these curtains for the kitchen," said Carla. "But when she hung them up she didn't like 'em and made white ones instead. So they're left over. They're yours if you want 'em."

The curtains would frame her display beautifully, thought Sarah. And there was more material than she needed for the side panels. She could lay some of the extra cloth on the window platform and place the loaves on top. It would look attractive and stylish.

"I brought pins," said Carla, "so we can tuck the curtains up to fit."

"That's wonderful!" cried Sarah. Then Carla reached into the box again and brought out a brown bag.

"What's that?" asked Sarah.

Carla grinned. "Our lunch."

As Carla was leaving, Sarah tore off a piece of the red-checked cloth. "Here." She handed it to her friend. "Put this in my lucky box for me."

"Why, for heaven's sake?"

"Just because I want to keep it." Leaving her box at Carla's could get to be a nuisance, she thought. Especially if her friend questioned her about everything she decided to put in it.

Carla took the swatch of cloth. "All right. It's your box. So long. See you tomorrow."

Sarah stepped outside to check the time on the court-house clock. Three-thirty. Mama would be coming with the bread soon. For more than one reason she could hardly wait. Maybe the postman had brought them good news.

Two weeks later there was still no news from Daddy. Sarah could tell that Mama was worried about him. So was she. But neither of them said much about it, and they worked harder than ever. Sarah sold bread and cinnamon rolls in Mr. Willard's building every afternoon from four to six. Since the store was located downtown, the bread sold well. The Willards had told her they were thrilled with the store's appearance. Mama had been delighted.

Sarah was usually left alone to sell, since Mama needed

97

the extra time at home. Most days Carla helped Sarah mind the shop. Between customers, Sarah often discussed her fears.

"Maybe your daddy found work and has been too busy to write," suggested Carla.

"But you'd think he'd tell us right away. He might be hurt or sick. I don't know what's going to happen, Carla. If Daddy doesn't find a job, he might not send for us."

"What would he do then?"

"I don't know. Just keep on going from place to place, I guess." She paused. "Carla, do you suppose that's how men turn into hoboes?" The words surprised her. She had never spoken them before, but had mulled them over in her mind many times.

"Gosh, I don't know, Sarah. I hope he comes back here, because I don't want you to move away."

"I wouldn't want to leave you either," said Sarah. "But if I move out West, maybe you could come to see me. On a train. Wouldn't that be fun? I bet we could climb a mountain together. The high kind, with snow on top. Or if we move to California, we could go swimming in the ocean."

"Yeah, that would be fun," said Carla. Then a customer came in, and their talk stopped.

One afternoon, a week later, Carla had left the store early for a music lesson. All alone, and with only two more loaves to sell, Sarah waited for her next customer. When she was by herself in the empty store, she often thought of Daddy. They still hadn't heard from him, and there were times now, at night, when Sarah heard Mama cry herself to sleep.

A few minutes passed and no one came in. Sarah picked up her broom and swept the floor where her customers had tracked in some dirt. Then she propped the broom against the door frame and sat down to finish her library book. She loved stories. While she was reading a good book her mind was too busy to think about Daddy. She hoped to sell her last two loaves soon and leave early. She wanted to borrow another book before the library closed.

Sarah heard someone open the door. When she glanced up, she saw a man standing in front of her. He looked like one of those tramps she had seen getting off the boxcars at the train station. He was a thin man, barely taller than she was. Several days' beard shaded his lower face, and his beaklike nose had been reddened by the hot sun. The sleeves of his dirty checked shirt had been torn off above the elbows. And he smelled bad. Like stale sweat mixed with — whiskey? She remembered the odor from the day they'd moved into their house, when Daddy had dumped the bottle near the steps.

"Could you spare a hungry man a free loaf?" He shifted a heavy-looking gunnysack from one shoulder to the other.

Probably everything he owned was in that lumpy bag, Sarah thought. Since Daddy was traveling around the country like that, Sarah found it hard to say no. She had to, she told herself. She couldn't spare a single loaf. But there were plenty of people in this town who would be glad to trade him a meal for a little work.

"I'm afraid I can't," she said. "But I know someone who'd give you something to eat." She wrote down the Petersons' address for him. "Two blocks east and three blocks south of here. But don't tell them I sent you." She smiled. "You may have to mow their grass or something."

"Thanks." He took the slip of paper and put it in the hip pocket of his frayed trousers. "You alone in here?" he asked.

"Yes," she said. When he grinned, she became suspicious. Why did he ask? She tried to cover her mistake. "But my mother will be coming back any minute."

"Your mother, huh?"

"Yes."

The man began to dig into his pockets. Was he searching for money?

"How much is one of them loaves?" he asked.

"Fifteen cents."

"You got change for a dollar?"

"Sure," she said with a smile. So he had money after all! From the floor beside her chair, she picked up the cigar box that held the day's earnings. When she opened it, he lunged at her and snatched it out of her hands. Then he spun around and dashed out the door.

13

c h a p t e r

SARAH SAT STUNNED, but only for a moment. How dare
he take her money! Her blood boiled. She bounded up
from her chair and grabbed the broom. Holding on to
something made her feel braver. Clutching it with one
hand, she bolted out the door.

There he was, walking down Main Street half a block
away. He was staggering a little. Drunk? Probably. The
nerve! He hadn't even bothered to run. He must have
thought that since she was a kid, she'd be too scared to
chase him. She'd show him a thing or two!

Running hard, Sarah dodged several people who got
between her and the thief. All she could think of was the
money. She had to get it back. Hadn't Daddy said she
shouldn't let people steal from her? That she should fight
back? And what would Mama say if she just sat there and
let someone steal a whole day's earnings? They couldn't
afford it. Catching up, she walked a step or two behind
the thief. In one hand he held the knapsack over his shoulder. And in the other he clutched her cigar box.

Should she hit him over the head with the broom? No,
she decided. It wouldn't hurt him very much. He'd probably just look back at her and run. Better to trip him the

way Daddy had taught her to do. If he fell it would give her time to get the box. Quickly Sarah thrust the straw part of the broom between his feet. As he lost his balance and fell forward, Sarah heard people around her gasp and yell. Some jumped out of the way. While he was falling, he let go of the big gunnysack. It flew open at the top and landed on the sidewalk at the same time he did. A frying pan and a tin cup tumbled out and clattered on the pavement near his head. But he was still gripping the money box. Why couldn't he have dropped it? She had to get it!

Before he could get up, she rolled his heavy knapsack over his head and shoulders. As he lay face down on the sidewalk, both his hands came up to pull the big bag off his head. At last he had let go of her money! Sarah whirled around and stomped her foot on the box. Still holding the broom, and never taking her eyes off him, Sarah backed away from the thief. The money box scraped against the pavement as she slid it under her foot. She had wanted to sneak the box away from him quietly.

Her thoughts raced. If she ran back to the store now, he might follow her. It would be better to fight him off right here, with people watching. She felt the murmuring crowd grow larger. The man rolled the bag off his head, got up on his knees, and stared at her for a second. Since he didn't seem to notice all the folks standing around, Sarah thought he surely must be drunk. With both hands she gripped the broom, straw side up, as if it were a baseball bat. The thief lunged at the box under her foot. But he didn't make it, because Sarah pushed the prickly end of the broom into his face. Hard. He yelled and toppled over on his side.

"You should be ashamed of yourself!" she shouted. By now a crowd of twenty or thirty people had gathered around them. Two men who stood nearby grabbed the thief, pulled him to his feet, and held him.

"Hey! Whatta you think you're doin'?" yelled one.

The other one shouted, "Someone call the sheriff!" But somebody else must have seen the start of the scuffle and called earlier, because the law officer drove up a second or two later.

"What's goin' on here?" he asked. The sheriff was a tall man with a squarish head.

"He stole my money," said Sarah. "He came right into my store and took it."

"You get your money back?"

Sarah opened the cigar box, and glanced at the dimes, nickels, and pennies inside. "I don't know for sure, but I think so."

"Heh! heh! heh! Good work," he said. Why was the sheriff laughing like that? Sarah wondered. She guessed it was because she was a kid. The officer handcuffed the tramp while the two men held him.

"You shoulda seen it," one of them said to the sheriff. "That kid there knocked this guy down and got the box. And she did it with that ol' kitchen broom. Easy as swattin' a fly." The thief rolled his eyes in disgust while the sheriff laughed as if it was the funniest thing he'd ever heard.

A minute or two later, when the law officer shoved the handcuffed man into the car, Sarah began to feel sorry for the thief. She remembered how it felt to be hungry, and called out to the sheriff.

"Are you going to give him something to eat?"

The officer turned to her and laughed again. "Shouldn't be any problem," he said. "He's gettin' to jail in plenty o' time for supper."

As Sarah watched the car drive off, several people came up to her and asked if she was all right.

"Sure," she said. Sarah ran back to the store with her broom over her shoulder and the money box tucked under her arm. She grinned as she listened to the coins jangle inside the box. Daddy would be proud of her, she thought.

Back at the store she counted her money, and was pleased that not a penny was lost. Soon people started pouring in, men and women who had seen the fight. Others who had only heard about it came too. Most praised her, saying she deserved a medal. But some said she should have been more careful, that she could have been killed. Suppose he'd had a gun? A gun! It hadn't even occurred to her. Then the mayor came in to meet her. The sheriff came too, and said he'd see to it that she got a certificate for bravery. He never stopped laughing. People from the newspaper dropped in to talk to her. One asked her questions and wrote down everything she said. Another took her picture.

"It was nothing much," she told them all. "He was just a little man. And he took my money." She couldn't imagine why everyone was making such a fuss. When she had done pretty much the same thing on the playground, her teacher punished her. She smiled and wondered what Miss Macmillan would have said if she'd seen this afternoon's fight.

At closing time Mr. Willard came into the store. Sarah was afraid he was going to bawl her out. After all, when she went out to catch the thief, she hadn't told Mr. and Mrs. Willard she was leaving the store as she was supposed to do. But Mr. Willard wasn't at all angry. Instead he handed her a key.

"You're a brave young lady," he said. "Mrs. Willard and I think it's time we trusted you to let yourself in and out."

Sarah took the shiny new key and held it in the palm of her hand as if it were a precious jewel. "Thanks, Mr. Willard."

At the door he turned to her. "By the way, if you ever need anything, Sarah, just let us know."

She beamed. The praise of the townspeople was such a joyful surprise.

At supper that evening Mama said, "I'm proud of you, Sarah. And your father would be too, if he were here."

Mama's mention of Daddy surprised Sarah. She took it as an invitation to talk about him, to unload her hopes and fears. "Mama," she said, "do you think he's going to send for us?" She studied the worry lines around her mother's eyes.

Mama said nothing. She just pushed her food around on her plate with her fork. She bit her lip and blinked, fighting tears.

"I'm sorry, Mama." Sarah felt a lump form in her throat.

"No, I understand." Mama's voice quavered. "We should talk about it. To tell you the truth, I can't guess what might have happened. And as long as we don't hear anything, we'll just have to assume he's all right."

Mama's birthday was one week away. Sarah was sure Daddy would write. He never forgot their birthdays. But since she didn't want to get Mama's hopes up, she said nothing about it. Instead she offered words of comfort. "Maybe Daddy wrote to us and his letter got lost in the mail."

Mama tried to smile, but her lips didn't quite turn up at the corners. "Maybe."

After supper Sarah walked down to a wooded place near the river. It was quiet and cool there, and she needed to think. She sat down on a log and watched a squirrel leap from one tree branch to another. What if Mama didn't hear from Daddy on her birthday? She'd need a special gift to cheer her up. But what could Sarah give her? She had no money of her own. The squirrel busily tore a twig from the tree. Sarah sighed, walked over to the river, and sat on the bank. A fish leaped out of the water and flopped back in again. She watched the rings spread out from the place where the fish went under. She had to think of something.

She got up and walked a short way downstream. Tiny plums grew on bushes near the bank. Sarah stopped to taste one. Nearly ripe. When they lived on the farm, Mama used to gather wild plums to make jelly. Her mother had taught Sarah how to cook the fruit and strain the juice and boil it with sugar to just the right stage. Mama loved plum jelly. Sarah had once taught her friends how to make it at a 4H meeting. Suddenly she knew what she had to give Mama for her birthday: plum jelly! It would be the perfect gift. They had some jars, but how could she afford the sugar? Aside from what they used for cinnamon rolls, they kept very little on hand. And she wouldn't be able to make it at home and keep the secret from Mama. She wanted it to be a surprise. The next day Sarah took her problem to Carla, who quickly found an answer.

Two days later, with the help of Carla and Mrs. Peterson, Sarah made a dozen jars of plum jelly in the Petersons' kitchen. Sarah and Carla had gathered the plums from the riverbank, and sneaked six jelly jars from the kitchen while Mama was out in the yard. Mrs. Peterson had provided the sugar, the rest of the jars, and the wax for sealing them. For these favors Sarah gave the Petersons half the jelly.

Sarah wrapped each of her six jars in newspaper and packed them into a box. When she reached home it took some doing to sneak the box into the house and hide it under her cot while her mother's back was turned.

When Mama's birthday came there was no letter from Daddy. Sarah couldn't believe that if Daddy were alive and well he would forget Mama's birthday. It wasn't like him. But her mother didn't say a word about it, so Sarah didn't mention it either.

The night before, when the oven was empty, Sarah had baked a chocolate cake to be eaten at supper that evening. And in the morning, when Mama opened her birthday package and found the six jars of jelly, she gasped with pleasure.

"How on earth did you do it?" she cried. When Sarah

107

told her, tears came to Mama's eyes. She hugged Sarah and said it was the most wonderful gift she'd ever had.

"I've been thinking," said Mama. "You need a little money of your own. How about fifteen cents a week?"

Sarah couldn't believe her ears. "Can we afford it?"

"I think so." Mama reached for the cracked sugar bowl, which she now hid behind the oatmeal box near the stove. Though she deposited most of their money in the bank, she kept a small amount in the bowl for what she called miscellaneous: little needs, like shoelaces and pencils.

Sarah cheered when Mama placed the coins in her hand. She felt as if it were her own birthday.

"You've earned it," said her mother.

But even on Mama's birthday it was business as usual. The two of them, carrying their sacks of bread and cinnamon rolls, pushed their way through the swarm of people waiting by the door. Sarah heard one of them shout, "Here comes the bread girl!" Since she caught the thief, folks had begun to gather in front of Willard's building each day, waiting for Sarah and her mother to open the shop. After the newspaper article came out, the crowds had doubled.

People poured into the store, pushing and shoving. It was hard to tell who was first in line. Even though Sarah and Mama had added two cents to the price of every loaf and packet of cinnamon rolls, their baked goods seemed more popular than ever. After the thief incident, Mama always stayed in the store with Sarah until their supply was sold out, which now took only a few minutes.

Sarah looked around the shop. The last loaf and roll had been sold, but people were still milling around inside. Sarah supposed they were waiting for more to be brought in.

"I'm sorry," said Mama, "we'll have to close now. We're all sold out."

"Awww!" some of them muttered.

"We'll be open again tomorrow," said Mama as people filed out the door. Sarah was glad to have a little free time. She wanted to go home and ice Mama's birthday cake. Maybe decorate it a little if she could find some wild flowers. She might even buy a package of little candles with some of the money in her pocket. If they cost only a nickel or dime, she'd still have money left.

A man stood in a far corner after the others had gone. He wore stained overalls and high shoes caked with mud. Sarah couldn't see his face because a torn straw hat was pulled down to shade his eyes; a gray-streaked beard and mustache covered his lower face. In one hand he carried a small gunnysack bundle, in the other a big bunch of garden flowers. Tramps didn't usually carry flowers, thought Sarah. What could he want?

As the man walked toward them, something about his stride seemed familiar. But that was ridiculous, thought Sarah. She had imagined seeing Daddy so many times that she no longer trusted such visions. Then she recognized him. Mama did too, in the same instant.

"Daddy!"

"Frank!"

14

chapter

AFTER THE HUGS and kisses, Daddy put an arm around
Sarah and handed Mama the flowers. "Happy birthday."

Mama held them and stared at Daddy. Tears streamed
down her cheeks. "You're alive! I was so afraid something
terrible had happened to you."

"Your beard and that hat fooled me, Daddy," Sarah
cried. "I didn't know it was you at first." She couldn't
believe that her father stood right there beside them, his
arm around her waist. It was too good to be true.

"Hey!" He glanced all around the store. "I see you're
running quite a business here. When I didn't find you home,
I came downtown. First person I asked knew where you
were."

"Daddy —" But Mama spoke before Sarah could get a
word in edgewise.

"We've done pretty well," Mama said. "With more
equipment and help we could do even better." She looked
down at the flowers. "Wherever did you get these, Frank?
They're gorgeous."

"On the edge of town." Daddy took off his hat, laid it on
the window display platform, and ran his fingers through

his hair. "Had to work for 'em though. I was walkin' along when I saw this pretty flower garden. I noticed the lawn needed mowin', so I knocked on the door and made a deal with the lady of the house. When I told her it was your birthday, she let me cut the grass for that bunch o' posies. And she threw in a sandwich too, but I ate that."

"Daddy!" Sarah cried. "Did you come to get us? Are you going to take us out West on a train?"

"Whoa! Slow down a little, Sarah," said Daddy. "I guess I'd better explain. I didn't have any luck finding steady work out West. So after I visit you here for a day or so, I'm gonna hop on another boxcar and head east. There has to be a good job out there somewhere for a man who's willing to work."

A frightened look swept the smile from Mama's face. "Frank, I can't believe that you'd try another trip like that when the first one brought you nothing." Sarah stared at Daddy. His arrival was like a summer mirage, meant only to tease and vanish.

"I have no choice," said Daddy. "What else can I do? I have to keep on looking. But I brought you something." He bent over, took off one of his boots, and pulled out several dollar bills. He handed them to Mama. "I managed to save a little from odd jobs here and there. I would have brought you more, but some tramp picked my pocket between here and Denver."

Mama took the money. "Thanks. There may be a good job waiting for you right here in Waheegan," she said. "That is, if you're willing to take it."

111

"What do you mean?" asked Daddy. "Did somebody offer me one?"

"Well, not yet." Mama glanced at Sarah and winked. "But I think someone will, very soon." Sarah thought she knew what Mama meant. Maybe they could talk him into staying and helping them make bread. Did she dare hope?

Daddy smiled. "Hey, tell me about it."

"Later, after supper," said Mama.

"Come on, Daddy." Sarah pulled his arm. "Let's go home."

"I could do with a shave and a bath," he said.

"And birthday cake with frosting?" asked Sarah.

"Cake?" Daddy raised his eyebrows. "You're kiddin' me! When I left we were lucky to have bread on the table."

"It's chocolate," said Sarah.

"Now you're talkin'. Let's go!" Since he seemed so happy to be with them, thought Sarah, he surely wouldn't want to leave again. They just couldn't let him go.

Sarah and Daddy were eating their second piece of birthday cake while Mama looked on, drinking a cup of coffee. During supper Daddy had told them about the mountains and ranches out West. And about the ocean off the California coast.

"Why did you stop writing to us, Daddy?" Sarah asked.

"I was working my way east again. I thought I'd be seein' you long before this, but the trains didn't always head in the right direction. When I could, I worked off and

112

on, a day here and a day there. Then, too, I was ashamed to be writin' bad news all the time."

"Bad news would have been better than none," said Mama. "We kept imagining the worst."

"I'm sorry." Daddy reached out and took Mama's hand. Then he glanced at what was left of their pork chop dinner. "You can't imagine what a relief it is to see you both doing so well. Congratulations. By the way, what's the job you were gonna tell me about?"

"There's a steady job waiting for you right here," cried Mama, "with us!"

Sarah crossed her fingers. Please, she thought, let Mama convince him to stay.

Daddy wore a half smile, as if he didn't quite believe Mama. "What do you have in mind for me to do?"

"You could help us with the baking and selling. And there are books to keep and supplies to order."

Daddy stared at his folded hands and rubbed one thumb over another. He said nothing.

"Well?" asked Mama.

"Some fellas I traveled with are going east," he said. "To Detroit, to look for jobs in the auto plants. If that doesn't work out, they're gonna try the steel mills in Pittsburgh. I've decided to go too." It seemed to Sarah that Daddy had already made up his mind.

Mama went to a stack of newspapers she was saving, picked up several, and placed them in front of Daddy. "Here's a picture of a bread line in Detroit. The eastern cities are harder hit than we are, Frank, and I'm sure Pitts-

113

burgh is no better. Here's an article about New York. Jobs are scarce everywhere. No matter how hard you try, Frank, you won't be able to run away from the Depression."

Daddy glanced at the papers and sighed.

Mama sat across the table from him and spoke in a quiet voice. "Sarah and I have a going business, Frank. For the first time since we moved to town, we're paying all our bills and have money to spare. Not much to spare, you understand, but a little." She went to the bedroom and brought out her handbag. She pulled out her bankbook to show him. "See? We have some money now, and all our bills are paid. But with your help we could run the business a lot better, I'm sure."

"Seems you're doin' all right, and I'm sure proud of you," said Daddy. "But I don't want to sponge off my wife and daughter. I'd feel like a fifth wheel. And when it comes to kitchen work, I'm afraid I'd be all thumbs."

"I could teach you how to bake bread," said Sarah.

Daddy shook his head. "Oh, I don't know about that. I'm apt to be a flop at bread makin', and you could end up wishin' you'd never asked me. When I was out on the road tryin' to heat up beans for my supper, I burned 'em more often than not."

Sarah felt it was time to put in her two cents' worth, just in case Daddy felt that cooking was a sissy thing to do. "Daddy, everybody should know how to cook. Men too. Most of the chefs in city restaurants are men. I've read about them in magazines at the library, and they make lots of money. Men work in bakeries all over the world. And in canneries, men put up all kinds of food. Cooking isn't just for women."

"All right, Sarah," said Daddy. "I understand what you're tellin' me."

Mama walked over to a shelf and picked up her account book. "Let me show you what our business looks like on paper." She went over the accounts and customer list with Daddy and explained how Sarah had gotten them the Willards' store. She also told him about buying their supplies through the flour mill.

Daddy nodded. "You're doin' very well. I'm proud of you both. By the way, I'm just curious. How much did Ed Schnabel give you for my gold watch?" Daddy was changing the subject, thought Sarah. It was a bad sign.

"Before I tell you," Mama said to Daddy, "I want to show you something." She reached into her purse again and held up Daddy's watch by its gold chain. She put it in his hands.

"You got it back," he cried. "I can't believe it!"

"No," said Mama. She explained that Mr. Schnabel had offered them only three dollars, and that she had refused it.

Daddy sat at the table, silent for a while. At last he spoke. "I'd like nothing better than to stay here with you two, you know that. But I don't want you to make a job for me just because you feel sorry for me. I couldn't stand that. And to tell you the truth, the idea of baking bread for a living would take some gettin' used to."

"I felt the same way," said Mama. "But Sarah dropped

115

this idea in our laps when we needed it most. It's all that stands between us and starvation. Believe me, I couldn't have done it without Sarah. After she starts school this fall, she won't be able to help much. I'll need a partner desperately, and if I took on another person, our profits could be cut in half. We'll have to keep the money in the family or go broke. We do need you, Frank. Surely you can see that." A serious look came over Daddy's face and he patted Mama's hand. Then Mama explained about how Sarah had saved them from the poorhouse.

When Mama finished, Daddy's eyes were damp. For a short time he said nothing. He just sat there staring at the watch in his hands, rubbing the monogrammed cover with his thumbs. At last he spoke in a hoarse whisper. "Teach me what I need to know. I'll try hard to pull my own weight."

The next morning Sarah showed Daddy how the temperature of the water for mixing the yeast had to be just right so that the bread would rise. Then she showed him how to mix and knead the dough. She noticed that he followed her directions very well. When it came time to punch down the dough, he molded it into a silly face, and they both laughed.

He had only one complaint. "I feel mighty silly wearin' this thing," Daddy said as he pulled at the apron he wore. Mama had lent him one of hers, with violets printed all over it.

"It helps to keep your clothes clean," said Sarah.

Mama, who had been bending over the oven, stood up. "I can make you a plain white one, Frank."

"Good," he said.

As they shaped the loaves, Sarah explained what she knew about rising dough. "In a way, it's growing. Like the wheat in the fields."

"I never thought of it like that," he said.

After a try or two Daddy was baking a very good loaf. Mama taught him about the oven and how she kept the books and ordered the yeast and wrapping paper. He learned very quickly and was soon helping them with every job in the business. As the last hot days of July melted into August, Daddy never again mentioned going east to find work.

15

c h a p t e r

ONE STEAMY AFTERNOON Sarah was taking the second batch of bread out of the oven while Daddy packed up the first. The shop opened in an hour. It had grown so dark in the kitchen that Sarah could hardly see. She pulled the chain to turn on the light.

Mama was wrapping cinnamon rolls in waxed paper, and glanced at the clock. "For three in the afternoon, it's getting mighty dark. A thunderstorm must be brewing." She looked out the window.

"Have to see what's goin' on out there." Daddy, wearing the new white apron Mama had made for him, stepped out the door.

Sarah followed him. She stood on the back step and looked up. Greenish clouds churned across the sky, and the air was still and hot.

Daddy turned to Sarah and smiled. "One look at hail clouds like that and I'm almost glad I don't farm anymore." Sarah squeezed his hand. She remembered how scared he used to get when it hailed. It meant he'd lose all his crops.

He patted Sarah's shoulder. "We'd better get back to work. Store opens at four."

Sarah wiped the perspiration from her forehead. The

damp heat clung to her like a heavy cloak and was making her feel tired.

As Sarah piled the last loaves into sacks, the wind began to shake the windows and swing the screen doors back and forth against the house.

Mama rushed to the back door. "I'd better hook those screens."

"I'll help you, Mama." Sarah ran through the front room. The darkness was deepening, crawling into all the corners like a spreading black monster. She reached for the front screen door, which was now flattened against the outside wall, and pulled it with all her might. The wind was so strong she had a hard time closing it. When she walked back into the kitchen, the roaring started. It sounded like a train, only louder. Mama was standing at the back door, shouting at Daddy, who must have gone out.

Sarah heard Daddy yell, "It's a twister! Get outa that house. It'll blow away!" Then Sarah stepped outside and saw it. She stood there hypnotized, her eyes fixed against the sky. In the distance the funnel cloud, bending and twisting, dipped down to the ground like a huge elephant's trunk. What would they do? They had no basement or storm cellar.

Daddy ran up, grabbed Mama and Sarah by the wrists, and pulled them toward the truck. "Get in," he said. "Let's try to outrun it. It's comin' from the southwest." Sarah, seated in the truck beside Mama, watched Daddy as he turned the crank, his forehead creased with fear. Sarah silently urged him on. Hurry, Daddy, hurry! The roar of the storm grew louder. It was gaining on them. Twice Daddy cranked the truck, but it wouldn't start. Glancing at the sky, he threw down the crank and opened the door. He grabbed Sarah's hand, and pulled her out.

"Hold on to Mama!" he screamed. "Don't let go! And both of you follow me. Hurry!"

Numb with fear, Sarah obeyed. She grabbed Mama's arm and pulled her out of the truck. Sarah gripped Daddy's hand, and with her fingers locked in Mama's, ran behind her father. Where were they going? she wondered. Daddy was leading them somewhere, running. It was all Sarah could do to keep up with him. Mama, who ran behind her, stumbled several times. Did Daddy know what he was doing, leading them out into the storm like this? Maybe they'd be better off in the truck. With all the dust and trash and leaves whirling around, Sarah couldn't see much. If they weren't holding on to each other, they'd surely get separated and lost. Daddy pulled Sarah and Mama a few more yards, into a ditch by the road. He got behind them and pushed them to a drainage culvert, a big concrete pipe connecting the ditches on either side of the road.

"You two crawl in," Daddy shouted.

"What about you, Daddy?" Sarah screamed.

"After you two. Hurry! And keep your head inside." He gave Sarah a strong shove that sent her wriggling into the pipe. She crawled to the far end. It was smart of Daddy to think of the culvert, thought Sarah. Mama came creeping in after her, her head behind Sarah's knees, and called out to Daddy. "Frank! Get in. Hurry!"

Sarah was deafened by what sounded like the roar of a

million trains. Her ears popped and her hands and feet tingled. Here it was, the worst of it. "Is Daddy in here?" she yelled to Mama. But she couldn't even hear her own voice. She pressed her hands against her ears to shut out the roaring, but the sound of the storm shook her whole body. She blinked away the dust in her eyes and looked through the opening at her end of the culvert. A whole tree was being yanked out of the ground as if by an invisible giant. A second later she saw their truck sail through the mud-colored air. And was that the roof of their house turning somersaults in the distance? What about Daddy? Had he crawled into the culvert in time, or had the storm swept him away, too? She looked back, but she couldn't see past Mama's shoulders.

"Please, God," she prayed, "let Daddy be in here with us." What a nightmare, she thought. Maybe she'd wake up soon, and everything would be all right. Then she and Carla would have a good laugh about it. Carla! Sarah hoped her friend was home and safe. At least the Petersons had a basement. She wondered if her lucky box would survive. Mama was shivering and sobbing as she held on to Sarah's legs. The storm was real, all right.

Still huddled in the culvert, Sarah took her hands away from her ears. The roar of the twister was dying down a little, and she could hear other sounds: ripping, splintering, and thudding.

"Are you in here, Daddy?" she yelled.

"I'm here," he said. "You all right, Sarah?"

121

"Sure, Daddy." How wonderful to hear his voice.

"You're not hurt are you, Frank?" asked Mama. "I thought I heard you cry out."

"Tree branch poked me in the leg before I got in. It's nothing. Don't get out yet. It's not over."

Daddy was right. Their hiding place shook as heavy objects crashed down on the road above them. What were they? Sarah wondered. She gripped Mama's arms, which still circled her legs, and the two of them trembled together. It sounded as if the world was breaking to pieces! Please, God, she silently prayed, let us all live through this.

After a minute or two things stopped falling. Through the culvert opening, Sarah saw a few big raindrops begin to splash down. The worst of it was over, and they were still alive.

Then Daddy shouted at them. "Sarah! Lucy! Crawl out straight ahead. I'll follow you. There's a tree down over here. Make it snappy. The rain'll flood us out in a minute."

Daddy's right, thought Sarah as she scurried out of the pipe. The rain was pouring down, and soon the culvert would fill with rushing water. They could drown if they stayed down there. Sarah turned and helped Mama out and onto her feet. Not a minute too soon, Daddy joined them. The three clung together as a curtain of rain swirled around them. They could see nothing. The ditch became a rushing stream, and they climbed up to the road. Arms locked, they stood there, soaked to the skin.

When the rain lightened, Sarah could see a bit. But what scrambled place was this? Nothing looked familiar. As far as she could see, all that was left of the nearby houses were pieces of jagged lumber and rubble. Trees and telephone poles, broken and splintered, lay everywhere. And where was their house? She was sure she was looking in the right direction. But . . . It couldn't be! The outside walls and roof had vanished. The floor was still there, and so was one inside wall with the cookstove attached to it. Relief flooded over her when she saw their big kitchen range. From where Sarah stood, it looked undamaged. But how could they bake without a house? The mulberry tree and the clotheslines near the back door had disappeared.

"Our house." cried Mama. "Look!" Daddy put one arm around her and the other around Sarah. In a minute or two the rain stopped. Then all around them, up and down the street, the screaming and crying started. Scary, heart-breaking sounds, some near, others farther away. They were lucky, thought Sarah. It was over and they'd lived through it.

"Stay right here," said Daddy. "I'm going to take a look."

"I want to go with you," cried Sarah.

"No. It's dangerous. Electric wires will be down. Stay right here until I come back to get you."

"Be careful, Frank," said Mama.

"I will."

Sarah kept her eyes on Daddy until he disappeared behind a pile of rubble. Suppose he became discouraged again and kept on going all the way to the train station? But surely he wouldn't go away again. He said he'd be back.

From the road Sarah and Mama stared at their yard.

"I wonder where my washing machine is," said Mama.

123

Sarah threw her arms around her mother and held her while she sobbed. But Sarah didn't cry. She wouldn't dare admit it to Mama, but the whole thing seemed strangely exciting. They were alive. They still had their cookstove. And they'd have to move away from that awful place.

After a few minutes Daddy came back to where they sat. Sarah heaved a sigh of relief. He hadn't left them.

"Stay right where you are," he said. "It's terrible. The sheriff may be on his way with people to clean up and lead us out of here. We should wait and not try to walk through it. There are some folks hurt down the street a ways."

"Is the whole town gone?" asked Sarah. She kept thinking about Carla and the Willards. Others, too.

"From what I heard," said Daddy, "this side of the railroad tracks was hit worst. But it's too soon to tell."

They wouldn't be able to open the store that afternoon, Sarah thought. And what had happened to all the bread they had baked? Was it still whirling around in the sky somewhere?

"What are we going to do, Frank?" asked Mama.

"I reckon people around here'll be stayin' in churches and schools until they can find homes somewhere."

"You won't take a train and leave us again, will you, Daddy?" Sarah hadn't intended to ask that question. The words just slipped out.

Daddy scratched his head. "What makes you ask that?" By answering with another question, Daddy hadn't calmed Sarah's uneasy feelings.

"Hope the storm didn't blow the bank away with all

our money in it," Daddy said. He'd changed the subject too, thought Sarah. Not exactly a good sign.

"If we'd left our money in the house, it would be gone for sure," said Mama.

If they took much time off from baking, Sarah thought, they'd starve. "Where are we going to bake, Daddy?" After she asked, she was sorry. Stupid question. How would Daddy know? And if he thought too much about the fix they were in, he might catch the next freight train east. He didn't answer.

"You didn't happen to see my washing machine, did you Frank?" Mama wiped her tears with the back of her hand, leaving smudges across her face.

"Nope, Lucy. I didn't. My truck's gone too." Daddy sat down beside them and buried his face in his hands.

Sarah put her arm around him and patted his shoulder. "You saved our lives, Daddy. If you hadn't shoved us into that culvert, I'll bet we would have been killed. And we still have our oven!" She looked down at his pant leg. It was torn and bloody. "Daddy," she cried, "you're hurt!"

"It's nothin' much. Darn tree branch caught me before I crawled all the way in."

Sarah's eyes filled with tears. Daddy had been brave to push them into the pipe first.

When the rescue teams came in, Sarah pointed out the cookstove to them.

"Please save it for us," she said. "We need it."

125

"Yes," said Daddy. "We run a bakery." Sarah squeezed his hand. He didn't sound like a man who was about to run away, but she couldn't be sure. If she asked him to promise never to leave them, he might be hurt, especially if he wasn't even thinking about it.

"Don't worry. The storm area will be guarded," one of the workers said.

"Daddy," said Sarah, "don't you think it's strange that the only thing left was the cookstove?"

"What's strange about it? It's heavy as a battleship and attached to an inside wall."

"I think it's a sign," she said, "that we should go on with what we were doing. All three of us."

Daddy smiled a little and rubbed his chin. "Well, Sarah, when you get to be older you don't set much store in folderol like signs." Nothing he said offered her any comfort.

Mama was talking to one of the workers. "If you happen to find a Maytag washing machine with an adjustable wringer, it's mine."

"And please," said Daddy, "look for my Model T truck. The license number is F-3842."

16

chapter

LATER THAT AFTERNOON Sarah, Mama, and Daddy, wrapped in prickly brown blankets, sat in the back of the rescue truck. As they bumped along the newly cleared road, Sarah looked away from the shocked and tearful eyes of the other passengers. She noticed, as they rode through their wrecked part of town, that several shacks were still standing. Like weeds in a plowed field, she thought, ready to send out their ugly seed to sprout again and again.

As the truck jolted across the railroad tracks, Sarah saw that big puddles dotted the courthouse square. Undamaged, the buildings on Main Street were still wet from the rain and looked washed and bright against the gray sky. Earlier the rescue people had said that the tornado destroyed only their section of town. The rest of Waheegan suffered only slight wind damage.

Sarah smiled. The bank was still standing. Their money was safe! Then she saw the Willard building. Untouched, thank goodness. She was now sure that the Petersons' home was all right, too. She couldn't wait to talk to Carla.

The truck, along with several others, stopped outside the

First Methodist Church. Ambulances, with red lights flashing, waited there, ready to take the badly injured to a nearby hospital. Several men from area newspapers were running around with their notepads and cameras, asking people questions and snapping pictures. The families of hurt and missing people were crying and yelling, and the injured moaned on their stretchers.

Some people were sent to a temporary shelter at the high school, but the Pucketts were herded into the basement of the First Methodist Church, along with others who had minor injuries. Benches lined the walls of the huge room, and folding chairs were set up. But folks kept coming in, and some had to stand. The crowd murmured, babies cried, and little kids chased one another. Sarah felt relieved that someone would look after the gash on Daddy's leg. The blood on his pants had become a dry, brown stain.

Soon Carla's father, Dr. Peterson, came in with his black bag and went behind some folding screens in a corner of the room. A woman wearing a Red Cross band on her sleeve walked around with a pad of paper, talking to people and taking notes. Daddy was one of the last ones she questioned. She then hurried behind the screens, coming out again after a minute or two to call a name. A man with a limp made his way behind the partition.

While they waited for Daddy to see the doctor, Sarah said, "Mama, may I go to the drugstore to call Carla? I'll be right back."

"You can try," said Mama, "but I hear the phone lines are down."

128

"Then let me go to her house. It's only a few blocks from here."

Before Mama could answer, Sarah saw Carla dash through the doorway and stop to look around with wide eyes.

"Carla!" Sarah ran toward her friend, and the two girls hugged each other.

"Are you all right?" asked Carla. "Are your parents here? They weren't hurt were they?"

"I'm fine," said Sarah, "and my folks are over there." She waved an arm in their direction. "Daddy's waiting for your father to look at a cut on his leg. He says it's not bad. And Mama's fine."

"What a relief!" cried Carla. "When I didn't find you at the high school gym, someone told me to try here. What about your house?"

"It's gone. Is yours all right?"

"It's fine. A few tree branches on the lawn. Your lucky box is still safe. It's good you left it with me."

"Hadn't you heard? Lucky boxes always stay out of storms." The two girls giggled.

"Where are your folks?" Carla pushed her eyeglasses up on her nose. "My mother wants me to ask them something." Sarah led her to where Mama and Daddy sat.

"Mrs. Puckett," said Carla, "my mother wants all of you to stay at our house until you find another place."

Mama glanced at Daddy. They smiled and nodded.

"That's mighty kind o' your family," said Daddy. "You're a real lifesaver, and from what I understand, that's nothin' new with you folks."

Mama took Carla's hand. "Tell your mother many thanks. We'll be there after we see your father."

"My mother will pick you up in her car," said Carla. "I'll run home now and tell her I've found you." Sarah was so pleased to be staying at Carla's house that she nearly forgot about being homeless. She and her parents owned nothing but the damp clothes on their backs, a few dollars in the bank, a cookstove, and a lucky box. What's more, her father hadn't promised not to leave again.

After Daddy saw the doctor, the Pucketts left the church building with Carla and her mother. They were about to get into Mrs. Peterson's car when Mr. Willard stopped them.

"I've been looking for you," he said to the Pucketts. "I'm mighty glad to see you up and about."

"We're fine," said Mama.

"I was worried about you," he said. "I want to show you something right now. You may not want to do it, but then it might work out for you."

"I hope it won't take long," said Mrs. Peterson. "These folks need to come home with me and put on some dry clothes."

"It'll take just a few minutes," he said. "Why don't you all come?" The five of them followed him to the Willard building, which was just around the corner. He unlocked the door.

"I can let you people live in the back," he said. "That is, if you don't find something you like better. And I'll charge you the same rent you were paying before, whatever that was."

"It was five dollars a month," said Daddy. "Not very much, I'm afraid."

"It'll be enough," said Mr. Willard. "Do you have a stove you can move in here?"

"Yes," said Daddy, "but nothing else."

"There are a couple of chimneys you can hook up to. Take your choice." Mr. Willard pointed to two brick columns on either side of the store.

What a wonderful offer, thought Sarah. The building not only had electricity and running water, but an inside toilet as well.

"It's a good solid building," said Daddy, "and it certainly would be convenient. We could take the bread right out of the oven and pop it in the window. We could keep longer store hours too." He looked at Mama. "What do you think, Lucy?" When she smiled and nodded, Daddy shook Mr. Willard's hand. "We're mighty grateful."

"It's settled then." Mr. Willard reached into the window and took away the FOR RENT OR SALE sign.

Sarah could have shouted for joy. At last she knew that Daddy wasn't planning to go away. Mr. Willard patted Sarah on the shoulder. "As far as I'm concerned," he said, "nothing is too good for this girl." Embarrassed, Sarah studied her wet shoes.

Mama stood in the center of the big room and looked all around. "I could string a curtain across the middle of the store for privacy," she said. "It's perfect."

Excitement bubbled inside Sarah. The building was ever

131

so much nicer than the horrible house they had been living in. She noted, too, that in spite of the afternoon's downpour, no water dripped from the ceiling. And one of the best things about the move, she thought, was that they'd be saying good-bye to Shantytown.

17

chapter

STANDING IN THE front part of the store, Sarah took a green print dress out of a big cardboard box. She held it against her chest. "Look, Mama," she cried, "my size! It's almost new, and it's really pretty."

"Try it on." Mama shook her head as she opened the flaps of another carton. "More groceries. I can't believe how good everyone has been to us."

Sarah ducked behind the curtain into the private part of the store. While she changed, she thought about the three days since the storm. It had been like Christmas. Boxes of groceries and clothing kept pouring in from all over town. Sheets and towels, too. And furniture: beds, dressers, and two small tables. Someone had even given them a discarded wood-burning cookstove. They now had two ovens — just what they needed. They'd be able to bake a lot more.

Sarah and Carla had helped Mama fix up the back of the store, while Daddy and Mr. Willard moved the cook-stoves in and hooked them up to the chimneys. They had already started to bake again.

Sarah came out from behind the curtain and twirled around to show Mama the dress.

"It looks nice, honey." Someone was knocking at the

door, and Mama walked over to open it. Through its long glass panel, Sarah saw a man standing outside. A truck was parked on the street behind him.

"Ma'am," he said, "I have a big table in my truck here. I thought since you folks were in the baking business, you might want it. It's been in our basement a long time and we don't need it."

"That's ever so nice of you," said Mama. "I'd be happy to take it, but I'll have to ask my husband and daughter what they think." Sarah followed the man outside while Mama went to get Daddy, who was kneading dough in the back. The table was lying on its side, and it was huge. It must be seven or eight feet long and at least four feet wide, thought Sarah. Strong looking, too, with its thick, swirled oak legs. They'd have to keep it in the front of the store since there wouldn't be room in back. But it would be just right for kneading dough. The tables they owned were too small.

Sarah smiled as Daddy came out, wiping his hands on his apron. A week ago you couldn't have paid him to step out on Main Street in an apron. Sarah guessed he'd been so busy he forgot.

"What do you think?" asked Sarah. "It would be perfect for kneading dough and shaping loaves."

"It looks good to me," said Mama.

Daddy shook his head. "I don't know. We don't have room for it in the back."

"But we could put it in front," said Sarah. "Those tables in back are too small."

134

Daddy frowned. "In front o' the big windows?"

"Why not?" Mama asked. "I don't care if people watch me make bread." She winked at Sarah behind Daddy's back. Though Daddy had never said a word about it, they both knew that he would rather people didn't see him work with dough. It was silly, thought Sarah, and the sooner he got over it, the better.

"Please, Daddy," Sarah cried, "let's take the table. Besides, the front of the store looks bare, and when the shop is open we can use the table as a counter."

Daddy nodded to the man and grinned. "Seems I'm outnumbered. Guess we'll take it. Mighty thoughtful of you. Here, let me give you a hand."

The two men placed the big dusty table in the front part of the store, in full view of the large show windows. With brushes and soapy water, Sarah and Mama scrubbed it down to its pale oak finish. Then they spread flour on top. Sarah took some of Daddy's dough from the back, brought it out to the big table, and started kneading it.

Soon a small crowd gathered in the street outside the window to watch her. When Daddy came out from behind the privacy curtain, Sarah expected him to duck behind it, but he didn't. When he saw all the people out there, he grinned and waved. Leaning over the table, he scrawled a message on a brown paper sack: OPEN AT NOON. He clipped it to the red-checked window curtain with a clothespin, then disappeared into the back of the store. A few seconds later he came out again with a big pan and set it down on the table between himself and Sarah. He grabbed some

135

dough and started kneading it. Sarah couldn't believe her eyes!

"You were right," Daddy said. "We needed this table." Once in a while he looked up and waved at the crowd on the street. "Pretty good advertising, wouldn't you say?" he asked.

"The best," said Sarah.

"Yep," said Daddy, "nobody's gonna say our bread isn't homemade. No sirree."

Mama looked on and smiled. A minute later she brought out a pan of dough and started making cinnamon rolls. "When we get settled in," she said, "I might try my hand at cakes and pies. Just a few at first, to see how they go. I used to be good at it."

"That would be wonderful," said Sarah.

"What do you think we oughta call our bakery?" asked Daddy. "Every business oughta have a name."

"Gee, I don't know," said Sarah. "I never thought about it."

"I have an idea," he said. "After all, Sarah, you won that blue ribbon at the fair a while back." He glanced across the table at Mama. "If it wasn't for our champ here, we might have ended up in the poorhouse. I think we oughta call it the Blue Ribbon Bakery."

Sarah grinned. Daddy must be proud of her to suggest that name. But to her, it didn't seem quite right.

"That's nice, Daddy," she said. "But I think we ought to call it Pucketts' Blue Ribbon Bakery. It's a family business now."

Daddy pronounced the name slowly, as if listening to the sound of it. "Pucketts' . . . Blue . . . Ribbon . . . Bakery. What do you think, Lucy?"

Mama nodded. "I like it. And I think we should display that ribbon you won, Sarah. We ought to put it in the window and let people know that our bread is made from your prize-winning recipe."

"You still have it?" asked Daddy.

"Sure. It's in my lucky box."

"Why don't you get it? Let's have a look at it," he said.

Sarah dashed behind the privacy curtain and took the wooden box out of her dresser drawer. She listened as Mama and Daddy talked.

"That girl sure pulled us out of the quicksand," said Daddy.

Mama sighed. "That's true, Frank. Who would have guessed that we'd be running a business in a few short months. And I just know that if we save our money we'll be living in a real house one of these days."

"You betcha, Lucy," said Daddy, "you betcha."

Sarah slid the top off her good luck box and dumped it out on the dresser. She picked up the small piece of red-checked cloth. It would always remind her of Carla's friendship and kindness. She glanced at the newspaper clipping telling all about how she'd caught the thief, and another story she'd cut out of the *Waheegan Sun* telling about the storm. It had been quite a spring and summer. Then she picked up the beautiful blue ribbon, shiny satin, with a fancy gold seal on it that said FIRST PLACE. A lot had happened since she'd won that prize. Most of it she'd rather not live through again. She parted the curtains and handed the ribbon to Daddy.

His eyes crinkled at the corners. "Do you have a pin, Lucy?"

"Of course." Mama disappeared behind the curtain and came out holding up a straight pin.

Daddy took it, knelt on the display platform, and pinned the ribbon on the red-checked window curtain. He glanced out toward the street. "That bunch o' gawkers must o' wandered off. Let's all go out there and see how it looks."

The three of them stood on the sidewalk and peered into the window. Sarah thought the shiny blue ribbon was beautiful against the red and white checks. She looked over at Daddy and saw a tear roll down his cheek. Here they were, thought Sarah, in that once-empty building on Main Street. After nearly starving and losing Daddy and just about everything else, they now had a store of their own.

"The ribbon looks good there," said Mama.

"Yep, it sure does," agreed Daddy. "And someday, when we get more money ahead, we'll put up a big sign. All the way across the storefront: PUCKETTS' BLUE RIBBON BAKERY." Daddy wiped his eyes on his sleeve. "Well, I s'pose it's time we stopped dreamin' and got back to work."

Sarah pulled him into the store. "We'd better hurry, Daddy, if we're going to open at noon."

138